TWILIGHT HEART

HARBINGER P.I. BOOK 7

ADAM J WRIGHT

I hadn't planned on spending a cold November night in a cemetery but here I was.

No one had hired me to be out here freezing my ass off but I'd noticed a news article about a strange event that had occurred at the Whispering Pines Cemetery and I'd felt duty-bound to check it out.

A couple of days ago, the police had decided to exhume the body of Mrs Linda Whittington, a woman who'd only been a resident of Whispering Pines for one week. Mrs Whittington had died at home in an apparent suicide while her husband had been on a business trip to Albany. At least that was what the police had been led to believe.

But recent evidence had come to light that placed the husband at home during the night his wife had died. Since she'd already been buried, a decision was made to exhume the body and search for evidence of murder.

The grave had been opened but the coffin had been found to be empty.

One side of the coffin had been splintered and broken and close examination had revealed scratch marks on the outside. The earth had been disturbed. Not the earth at ground level but the earth at the level of the coffin, six feet under.

It was as if something had burrowed into the coffin and taken Mrs Whittington's body away.

That left the medical examiner and the police scratching their heads in disbelief and confusion. They couldn't explain what had happened.

That was to be expected; they were regular people with no belief in the paranormal. They couldn't be expected to recognize the work of a ghoul.

Instead of enlightening them--and thereby tipping them off to the fact that hideous creatures like ghouls actually existed--I'd decided to deal with the subterranean grave robber quietly while everyone else slept.

So here I was, creeping around Whispering Pines in the dead of night, casting my flashlight beam around the small cemetery in search of Linda Whittington's tombstone.

The flashlight was in my right hand. In my left, I held a shovel.

Digging my way into the ghoul's tunnel was going to be hot work so, despite the cold, I wasn't wearing a jacket. Instead, I wore a black tee and a dark blue flannel shirt. Black jeans and boots completed my ensemble and ensured my clothing was dark enough that I wouldn't be seen from the nearby road. I doubted anyone would be driving past here in the dead of night but I wasn't taking any chances.

An enchanted dagger hung from my belt in a leather sheath.

There was no point bringing a larger weapon —a sword, for instance—because I was probably going to have to kill the ghoul inside one of its tunnels and a long weapon might snag on the walls or low ceiling. The dagger would give me better maneuverability in a tight area while still packing enough punch to kill the beast.

My light finally came to rest on the stone that bore Linda's name. The grave hadn't been filled in again after the discovery of her vacant coffin and was covered by a green tarpaulin that had been staked into the earth around the hole.

I lifted it off and dragged it aside. The empty grave beneath my feet was lost to darkness. I shone my light down there and examined the earth. I could see a section of earth that looked as if it had been disturbed recently. That would be the way into the ghoul's tunnel.

Climbing down into the grave, I remained alert for the slightest sound or movement. Ghouls generally avoided human contact but they'd fight and kill if cornered and had long claws and teeth with which to carry out the deed.

The air in the grave was cold. I thrust my shovel into the disturbed earth, eager to get to work so I could keep warm. When this was done, I was going home to a long, hot shower.

The earth gave way to the shovel blade easily and after a few minutes it collapsed, revealing a tunnel beyond. I shone the light into the tunnel and saw that it led into the earth for about twenty feet before branching both left and right.

Great, I was about to climb into a subterranean maze. I just hoped there was only one ghoul down here. With so many tunnels heading in different directions, it would be all too easy to find myself flanked by the damned things.

I took comfort in the knowledge that ghouls were usually solitary creatures. That didn't mean there couldn't be more than one in these tunnels but it was unlikely.

Still, I couldn't allow myself to become complacent.

The tunnel wasn't large enough for me to

stand up in but the ceiling was high enough to allow me to crouch.

Leaving the shovel in the empty grave, I unsheathed my dagger and climbed into the tunnel. The blue glow from the dagger, along with the bright beam of the flashlight, lit my way.

A fetid smell lingered in the air and seemed to cling to me as I proceeded deeper into the tunnel.

When I reached the intersection that led left and right, I decided to take a right. There was no logical reasoning behind my choice other than the fact that the right hand tunnel led deeper into the cemetery where the one that went left led toward the road.

I guessed that the ghoul's nest would be far away from the road and more likely to be situated at the rear of Whispering Pines, where the cemetery gave way to the pine woods that gave the place its name.

Moving forward in a crouching position made my thigh and calf muscles ache so I dropped into a crawl and made my way carefully forward. No point risking cramped muscles, especially down here. I needed to be in peak condition when I finally came face to face with the resident of this underground maze.

The deeper I went, the worse the smell got. After a couple of minutes, I was almost gagging on the stench of rotted flesh. It got so bad, I wasn't sure I could go any further.

Maybe I wouldn't have to. I could hear a scrabbling sound in one of the tunnels ahead. Something was coming this way.

And then my phone began to buzz in my pocket.

I couldn't imagine that anyone would be calling me at this time of the night unless it was an emergency. The scrabbling ahead sounded far enough away that I'd have a chance to at least check who was calling before the creature reached me so I dropped the flashlight and dug the phone out of my pocket.

Felicity's name was on the screen.

The sound in the tunnel was getting closer.

I backed up slightly and answered the call. The flashlight illuminated the tunnel in front of me so I'd know as soon as the ghoul appeared. I should have enough time to find out if Felicity needed me urgently. If she did, I'd back up all the way out of the tunnel and go help her. The ghoul could wait. It wasn't going anywhere.

"Alec," she said as I held the phone to my ear. "Are you there? The line's a bit crackly."

"I'm here," I told her. "I'm in a tunnel."

"A tunnel? I thought you'd be in bed. It's--"

"Yeah, I know how late it is. What's up?"

The scrabbling sound had stopped. Maybe the

creature was biding its time or maybe my light had put it off. Either way, I couldn't hear it moving toward me anymore. I hoped I wasn't going to have to go chasing it deeper into this underground warren; I wasn't sure I could handle the smell if I had to go any further.

"I've received an email," she said. "From the Society. I was wondering if you've received one as well, since its contents concern you as well as me."

"An email? I have no idea. Like I said, I'm in a tunnel right now."

There was a pause, during which I was sure Felicity was wondering if she'd heard me correctly. "You mean you're driving through a tunnel?"

"No, I'm not on the road. I'm in a tunnel underneath a cemetery."

"What are you doing there? It's--"

I didn't hear the rest of what she said because the wall next to me exploded outward and a snarling ghoul leaped forward, razor-sharp teeth and claws bared.

I dropped the phone and raised the dagger. The blade bit into the ghoul's shoulder and the creature wheeled away from me with a high-pitched shriek of pain. It huddled in the flashlight beam and put one huge paw up to the wound I'd given it.

If I'd thought the smell in the tunnels was bad, the stench coming off the creature was a thousand times worse.

It was ugly too, with an elongated snout that held hundreds of fangs and beady eyes that glared at me with a fiery hatred. Its body was covered with patchy brown fur and its ears were pointed like a bat's.

The beady eyes sized me up, flickering from my face to the glowing dagger in my hand. If it ran, I was going to have to chase it. If it attacked, I was going to have to defend myself and try to hold onto the contents of my stomach because the foul smell coming off the creature made me want to vomit.

I wasn't sure where my phone had landed but I heard Felicity's distant voice coming from somewhere. "Alec? Are you there?"

The ghoul hurled its body forward, arms and claws outstretched. Instead of backing away or waiting for it to land on me, I pushed forward with my legs and straightened my right arm--the one holding the dagger--while flinging my left arm behind me for balance. I lunged at the ghoul like a fencer striking a winning blow and felt the dagger penetrate the creature's chest.

Hot blood poured out of the wound and over my hand but instead of recoiling in horror, I pressed the blade deeper.

The ghoul's deadly teeth snapped at my face. Bringing my left arm forward, I elbowed the snout away and forced the creature against the tunnel wall, still plunging the dagger into its body.

The creature's eyes stared into mine for a second but the hatred they held faded away along with the ghoul's life force. Its body went limp and the flow of hot blood that had been pumping out of its body stopped when the heart finally gave up.

I pushed myself away from the corpse and backed out of the tunnel, finding my phone buried beneath a covering of dirt as I made my way back to the intersection that led to the grave.

Despite my lungs burning and my heart pounding in my chest, I didn't dare to take a deep breath until I was back in the open grave where the air tasted fresh and sweet. Once I was there, I leaned against the earthen wall and breathed in lungfuls of the cold night air.

Not only was I going to have to take a shower when I got home, I was going to have to throw these clothes into the trash. My shirt and jeans were covered in ghoul's blood and I was sure the stench that pervaded the tunnels had permanently embedded itself into the fabric of everything I was wearing.

I checked my phone to see if Felicity was still

on the line but the screen was dead. The phone must have gotten buried during the scuffle with the ghoul and some dirt must have found its way inside.

Great. So now I had no idea what email Felicity had been talking about and wouldn't know until I got home.

I couldn't leave the cemetery yet, though; there was one more thing I had to do.

I climbed out of the grave and made my way to the Land Rover, removing my blood-covered shirt, despite the cold. I opened the Rover's tailgate, threw the shirt inside, along with the useless phone, and took out a large plastic bottle of lye.

Returning to the grave with the lye, I entered the tunnels again and crawled to where the ghoul's body lay motionless in the beam from the flashlight.

I opened the bottle and poured the entire contents of lye crystals over the corpse. Ghouls are attracted to dead human flesh and they're even more attracted to dead ghoul flesh. If the body was left here to rot naturally into the earth, it would bring more of the damned creatures to the area.

Using lye to dissolve the body was an old Society trick I'd learned years ago. No one was sure exactly how it worked but a ghoul corpse covered in lye didn't attract the attention of other ghouls.

When I was done, I grabbed the flashlight and left the tunnel. I used the shovel to fill in the tunnel before climbing out of the grave and replacing the tarp over the hole. No one would ever know I'd been here. The only witness to my presence here was currently being dissolved by sodium hydroxide.

By the time I'd stowed my gear in the back of the Land Rover and climbed behind the wheel, I regretted the fact that I hadn't brought a change of clothing with me. I felt filthy and I was stinking up the car.

I drove home with all the windows open.

2

An hour later, I was standing at the kitchen sink, tapping my phone as I tried to dislodge the dirt from it.

I was freshly-showered and wearing a black T-shirt and sweats. The clothes I'd worn to the cemetery had been thrown out. After some fiddling with the phone, I managed to get it to switch on. While it booted up, I took it into the living room, where my laptop sat on the coffee table.

I checked my email but I didn't have anything from the Society so whatever communication Felicity had been talking about had been sent to her only.

While I was pondering that, the phone booted up completely and I saw that I had half a dozen missed calls from Felicity. Picking up the phone, I called her back.

"Alec," she said when she answered. "Are you all right?"

"Yeah, I'm fine," I said. "Sorry we got cut off. My phone kind of got buried. What's this email about?"

"Don't you have one too?"

"No, I just checked. Nothing from the Society. What does it say?"

There was a pause and then she said, "Can I come over and talk to you? I'd rather speak face to face."

"Of course. The door's unlocked. I'll make coffee." Remembering Felicity's beverage of choice, I added. "And tea for you."

I ended the call and went into the kitchen to make the drinks. While I was filling the coffee machine and waiting for the microwave to heat the tea, Felicity arrived. She was wearing blue jeans and a white T-shirt and an expression on her face that seemed torn between joy and sadness. The corners of her mouth were quirked up as if she were trying to hold back a smile but her dark eyes were filled with tears. I couldn't tell if they were tears of joy or sadness.

"Hey," I said. "What's the Society been emailing you about?"

"They've offered me a job," she said.

"A job?"

She nodded excitedly. "My own office. My own cases. They want to make me a fully-fledged P.I."

"Wow, that's great! I knew it wouldn't be long before they realized how great you are. I'm really pleased for you."

The microwave dinged but I ignored it. "Why are we drinking coffee and tea? We should be celebrating. I'm sure there's a bottle of champagne around here somewhere. Someone brought it to the Halloween party and it never got opened." I opened one of the cupboards and searched for the booze.

"There's something else," Felicity said. "The job is in Manchester."

I felt my heart sink a little. I'd been so excited for Felicity that I hadn't thought about the fact that her promotion meant she'd be leaving. I pushed my emotions down. This was everything Felicity had ever wanted and worked toward and I wasn't about to ruin her happiness by dwelling on the negative part of her big news.

"Manchester isn't far from here," I said. "We'll probably have some cases that intersect. I'm sure monsters cross the border between New Hampshire and Maine all the time."

She shook her head. "Not Manchester, New

Hampshire, Alec. The job is in Manchester, England."

"Oh," I said, pulling the bottle of champagne from the cupboard. I tried not to let the disappointment I felt show in my face or voice. "Well, that doesn't matter. What matters is that you're going to be a P.I. You've done it! Congratulations!"

I got two glasses and popped the cork off he champagne bottle. Most of the effervescent liquid spilled out onto the floor. I quickly poured what was left into the glasses and handed one to Felicity.

"To Felicity Lake, P.I." I toasted, clinking my glass against hers. We drank. I'd never been a fan of champagne and this glass wasn't going to change my mind. I set it aside and poured some coffee from the pot. After what I'd been through tonight, I needed the caffeine hit.

Felicity also put her glass aside and took the tea out of the microwave. "I'll never understand why you make tea in the microwave," she said as she placed the cup on the counter. "That's one thing I won't miss when I move back to England."

"But you'll miss some things, right?" I asked.

She nodded and her eyes became watery again. "Of course. I'll miss a lot of things."

"You've been invaluable as a colleague," I told her. "When do you start your new job?"

"In a couple of days. So I need to pack a bag and then catch a flight to London tomorrow evening. The Society will sort out the rest of my things and ship them over to England."

"Wow, that's fast." The reality of the situation hit me like a ton of bricks. Felicity was leaving tomorrow. Forever.

"So I won't be able to help with the lifting of Mallory's curse," she said. "I'll leave you all my research, of course."

"It's a shame you won't be here. It's only because of your research that we can help Mallory at all."

"You'll have to let me know how it goes," she said. "I mean, we're going to stay in touch, aren't we?"

"Of course we are. That is if you still have time to speak to me when you're a fully-fledged P.I."

"I'll make time."

"Good. That's settled, then." I finished my coffee and placed the cup on the kitchen counter. "We should have a farewell party. I'm sure everyone will want to say goodbye to you."

The sadness returned to her eyes. "There isn't time, Alec."

I ran the logistics through my head. If Felicity was going to be packing tomorrow and leaving in the evening, there probably wouldn't be time for a party. But I couldn't let her go without a proper send off; she was too important to just slip away.

"There's no need for any fuss. I'll make sure I say my goodbyes to everyone individually tomorrow," she said.

"Okay. Will you need a lift to the airport?"

"The Society is taking care of that. They're sending a car for me. My Mini will be shipped over to England later."

I nodded. When I'd moved here from Chicago, the Society had dealt with transporting my stuff to the new house. Everything had been done quickly and efficiently. That had been great at the time but now I was seeing another side of the Society's efficiency; everything happened so fast. Felicity would be gone tomorrow and her house would probably be empty the day after that.

There would be no lingering goodbyes, no time to say things that were still unsaid. Felicity's departure would be carried out with the speed and precision of a military operation.

She finished her tea and said, "I suppose I should go home and pack. You know what I'm like; once I know a job needs to be done, I can't rest until it's finished."

"Your efficiency is legendary," I told her, keeping my voice light and breezy. The office was going to be a lonely place without her.

She went to the front door and I followed.

"I'll come and say goodbye properly tomorrow," she said.

I nodded. "Of course."

She opened the door. Cold night air crept into the house.

"Until tomorrow, then." She stepped outside and walked down the driveway to the sidewalk before turning toward her own house. It would have been quicker for her to simply walk across my lawn to her own property but Felicity never did that. She always used the driveways and the sidewalk.

I stood at my door, shivering slightly in the icy air as I watched her make her way to the house that would be her home for one more night. When she got to the front door, she waved at me and disappeared inside.

I remained there for a moment, gazing out at the quiet street. Soon, the Mini parked on the driveway next door would be gone, the house empty.

Thanks to the Society's brutal efficiency, it would be as if Felicity had never lived here at all.

3

When I woke up the next morning, a heavy rain was streaking down the windows, blurring my view of the street. I showered and dressed quickly, putting on a red flannel, white tee, and jeans before heading down to the kitchen.

After Felicity's visit last night, I'd hardly slept at all and now I needed coffee to wake me up.

I turned on the machine and waited impatiently for the coffee to fill the pot. While I was waiting, a heavy knock sounded on the door. I answered, expecting to see Felicity outside but my heart fell when I saw Merlin, in Sheriff Cantrell's body, standing on the stoop.

"Alec," he said cheerily. "Are you ready for today's practice?"

I groaned, both inwardly and audibly. I'd

forgotten that I'd agreed to practice with Excalibur today. Merlin and I had come to an agreement; he'd help with lifting Mallory's death curse but in the meantime, Leon was going to analyze the computers we'd taken from a Midnight Cabal yacht and I was going to practice with Excalibur.

A couple of days ago, I'd told Merlin to come over today for a practice session but that was before I'd spent a night in a cemetery and then been given the news that Felicity was leaving.

"Not today, Merlin" I said as he pushed past me and went into the kitchen. He found a mug in the cupboard and filled it with coffee from the pot. He may have been living in the modern world for a while now but he still had a lot to learn about manners.

"What do you mean not today?" he asked after taking a sip of the coffee.

I poured some for myself and said, "I was up all night hunting a ghoul. I'm in no mood to play with that damned sword today."

"Play?" he asked, raising an eyebrow. "We're not playing, Alec. We're preparing to take down an evil cabal. You need to get to grips with Excalibur. You can't give up just because you're tired."

"I'm not giving up. I'm just postponing our

practice session. We can do it in a couple of days' time or even tomorrow but not today. I have other things on my mind today."

He scoffed. "What other things?"

"Felicity is leaving today."

He frowned. "What do you mean she's leaving?"

"She's going back to England. She has a new job."

"I thought she was helping your friend Mallory get rid of the curse."

"She was but now she isn't. We're going to have to do the curse thing without her."

"Oh. That isn't good. Her absence could greatly hinder us. It was Felicity who did all the research and---"

"Yes, I know," I said, cutting him off. "But we're just going to have to deal with it, okay? We don't have a choice."

"All right, there's no need to get angry."

"I'm not angry."

He took another sip of the coffee. "I can see you're upset. You need to keep your head in the game if we're going to lift Mallory's curse and then defeat the Midnight Cabal."

"My head is in the game," I told him.

"Are you sure?"

"Yes."

Seemingly satisfied with my answer, he finished his coffee and said, "So what are we going to do today? You don't want to practice with Excalibur but we have to do something productive."

I didn't feel like doing anything today other than sitting on the couch and sulking but I knew Merlin was right; we wouldn't get anywhere by doing nothing and we had a job to do. Mallory was depending on us.

"Okay, I'll get the gang together and we can decide on a course of action." If I got everyone over here, I could kill two birds with one stone by making progress towards helping Mallory and also throwing a small farewell party for Felicity.

She was going to be bringing her research around here later anyway, so some food, drink, and good company wouldn't hurt. Seeing everyone she knew would hopefully make her last day on the job more pleasant.

"Excellent," Merlin said. "The sooner we lift the curse from your friend, the sooner we can get on with the task of destroying the Midnight Cabal."

"And the sooner you can go back to where you came from and give Sheriff Cantrell his body back," I reminded him.

"Yes, yes," he said, waving my words away. "I

told you I'll let the sheriff back into his body when the Cabal is no more. You seem to doubt my word."

"It isn't that I doubt your word," I said, though in truth I wasn't sure if I could trust Merlin or not. "It's just that I don't think the sheriff should be trapped in an enchanted sleep inside a magical ice cave for any longer than he needs to be."

"I agree," he said. "He will awaken from the sleep as soon as we defeat the Midnight Cabal."

"And you'll willingly go back to the cave?"

He nodded solemnly. "Of course."

I still didn't believe him but there was no point dwelling on that now. Merlin needed Cantrell's body while we worked on taking down the Cabal. If he refused to leave after that, then that was something I was going to have to deal with later. Right now, though, a reminder here and there that he had agreed to return to the cave didn't hurt.

"I need to go to the store. We're going to need some food and drinks for later."

His face lit up. "Are we having another party?"

"Yeah," I said. "While I'm gone, I want you to call everyone and tell them to be here at noon. Can you do that?"

He nodded enthusiastically. "Of course."

"You probably don't have everyone's numbers

in your phone so just ask Amy, your daughter. I mean the sheriff's daughter."

"I can do that. She's at the station. I'll go there right away."

"Excellent." I ushered him out of the front door and into the rain. "See you later."

I grabbed my jacket and went out to the Land Rover. As I climbed in behind the wheel, my phone buzzed. Mallory's name appeared on the screen.

"Hey, Mallory."

"Alec, you need to--" Her words were cut off by static. "--here. There's something--" More static.

"Mallory, I can't hear you," I said. "I'm on my way."

I threw the phone onto the passenger seat. Damn thing must have been more affected by the cemetery dirt than I'd thought.

I had to wait for Merlin to move his patrol car because he'd parked it directly behind the Land Rover. When he finally got out of my way, I backed out onto the street and followed him toward town. When he stopped at the police station, I continued through town toward the highway.

Mallory was staying at a motel just outside of Dearmont called the Pleasant Pines. I'd told her she was welcome to stay in my guest room for as long as she wanted but she'd said she needed some solitude. She'd spent a long time alone in Shadow Land and she was finding that interacting with people was leaving her drained and desperately in need of time alone.

Or at least as alone as she could be with the spirit of an ancient Egyptian sorceress residing inside her.

I drove past Dearmont Donuts and glanced up at my office window. The lights were burning.

Maybe Felicity was in there, collecting some of her things.

I drove out of town and got onto the highway. The rain was coming down harder now, the sky a deep gray. I turned on the headlights against the gloom and increased the speed of the wipers. The rain buffeted the Land Rover with a force that made it seem as if the elements themselves were trying to stop me from reaching my destination.

Due to the weather conditions, the traffic on the highway had slowed to a crawl. I had to hit my brakes to match the speed of the other cars.

At least it wasn't far to the Pleasant Pines. Five minutes later, I was pulling into the motels parking lot and parking next to the Chevy Blazer that Mallory had rented from Earl's Autos a little farther along the highway.

Mallory was already waiting at the door when

I slid out of the Land Rover and sprinted through the rain toward her room.

"I couldn't hear you on the phone," I said. "What's up?"

"It's easier to show you," she said, leading me into the room.

The room was like any motel room; a simple space fitted with a double bed, nightstand, and small table. But on the wall above the bed's headboard, a series of hieroglyphs had been drawn with a black marker. In the middle of the ancient symbols there was a crude drawing of two pillars. The pillars were fashioned in the lotus style of ancient Egypt and each bore yet more hieroglyphs.

"Did you do this?" I asked Mallory.

She shrugged. "If I did, I don't remember it. It was there on the wall when I woke up this morning." She frowned. "What I mean is, I don't remember doing it. You know what I'm saying, right?"

I nodded. "You're saying Tia did this."

"Yes. She took over my body while I slept and drew these things on the wall."

"Do you have any idea what they mean?"

She shook her head. "No."

I took photos of the drawings on the wall with my phone and then asked Mallory to do the same in case my phone decided to die completely.

"I'm sure Felicity will know what they mean," she said after she'd finished taking a few shots of the symbols.

"Yeah," I said. "We can ask her later. Everyone's coming round to my place for a farewell party."

"Farewell party?"

"Felicity is leaving. She's got a job as a P.I. in England."

"Oh, wow. I'm pleased for her."

"Yeah, me too."

She put an arm on my shoulder. "Are you okay? I know how much Felicity means to you both as a colleague and as a person."

"Yeah, I'm fine. I'm really pleased that Felicity finally has what she's always wanted. She deserves it."

Mallory nodded. "Yes, she does, but that doesn't mean you can't be sad about her leaving."

"I know," I said, "but I'm not going to spoil her last few hours here by being depressed. You want to help me get everything ready for the party?"

"Of course." She took her jacket from the closet and followed me out into the rain.

When we were in the Land Rover, she checked the photos she'd just taken on her phone.

"Why do you think Tia drew that stuff last night?" I asked as I backed out of the parking

27

space. "She's been inside you for a long time so why now?"

Mallory shrugged. "She knows we're trying to lift the curse. Maybe she's trying to help."

I turned on the wipers. The rain seemed to be coming down even harder now.

I drove back to Dearmont through the pouring rain and when we passed my office, the lights were still on.

"Is Felicity in there?" Mallory asked when she saw me checking out the lit window.

"Maybe," I said. "I think she might be packing up some stuff."

When we parked outside the grocery store, I decided to call Felicity. Something about the lit window was bugging me.

"Alec," she said. "I went over to your house earlier to give you my research but you weren't in."

"I'm in town, getting groceries. I invited a few people over for a little get-together at noon."

"Oh, it would be nice to see everyone. I thought I'd have time to visit them separately but I've been so busy packing."

"So you're still at home?"

"Yes, of course. Where else would I be?"

"You haven't been to the office?"

"No. There isn't really anything there that I need to take with me today."

28

"Okay, cool. So I'll see you at noon."

"Yes, of course. See you then."

I ended the call and turned to Mallory. "We need to go by the office."

She nodded. "Felicity isn't there, is she?"

"No, she isn't. But someone is."

4

I pushed through the street level door of my office building and ascended the stairs with Mallory close behind me. The door was unlocked and hadn't been forced open so someone had either picked the lock or used some other means to gain entry without breaking in.

At the top of the stairs, all of the lights were burning. My office door was closed but the door marked Assistant, the door of Felicity's office--Felicity's old office, I reminded myself--was open. The rich smell of coffee hung in the air. I wasn't sure why someone would break into the building and make a drink but that seemed to be what someone had done.

With my muscles tensed and ready for action, I entered the office, staying low in case the intruder decided to take a swing at me with a weapon.

No attack came in my direction. A short, clean-cut man dressed in a cream-colored shirt, dark blue tie, and black trousers stood at the coffee machine. When he saw me, his face registered surprise and he almost dropped the cup he was holding.

He didn't look like a burglar, unless burglars were wearing shirts and ties these days. Nor did this guy look like any sort of threat. His thinning black hair and the lines on his face placed him in his late-forties and it looked like he'd spent most of his life in a sedentary job. He had a slim build except for a slight pot belly that pushed at the buttons of the shirt above his belt. Despite the belly, he looked like a strong wind could blow him away.

"Mr Harbinger," he said with a smile. It wasn't a question. He seemed to know who I was, which was more than I could say regarding him. Judging by his accent, he was Canadian but that was all the info I could glean at the moment.

"Who the hell are you and what are you doing in my office?"

He frowned. "Didn't you get the message? The Society was supposed to send a message to you about my arrival. I'm sorry." He placed the mug next to the coffee machine and came toward me with his hand outstretched. "I'm Carlton Carmichael, your new assistant."

We shook. His grip was weak, his hand dry. The Society hadn't wasted any time in replacing Felicity. That was odd since they usually dragged their heels when it came to such matters.

His gaze drifted to Mallory and he gave her a smile before offering her his hand. "And you're Mallory Bronson. Hello, nice to meet you. Carlton Carmichael."

The fact that he recognized Mallory and had recognized me meant that he must have seen photos of us before coming here.

He turned his attention back to me. "I guess this must be a shock for you, finding me here. I came by hoping you'd be here but the place was locked up. I have a key, of course, so I let myself in and acquainted myself with my new office. I hope that's okay."

"I had no idea you were coming," I told him.

He sighed exasperatedly. "I was told you'd be sent a text message."

"My phone isn't working properly; it's full of cemetery dirt."

He seemed taken aback by that for a moment and then he said, "Would you like me to take a look at it for you?"

"No."

"Okay, how about a drink? Coffee?" He

indicated the pot on the burner. "Or tea?" He pointed at the box of tea bags next to the machine.

"Those belong to Felicity," I told him, taking my phone out of my pocket and checking the texts. There was a message from the Society, even though the phone hadn't notified me. The message was simple and to the point, as most of the Society's messages tended to be.

New assistant Carlton Carmichael arriving today.

"I have a message about you," I told Carlton, "but it doesn't tell me anything other than your name."

"Then allow me to give you some details about myself. I hail from Renfrew, Ontario, and I've been working with the Society in Canada for fifteen years. I can speak seven different languages, including Old Norse and Enochian. Unlike your previous assistant Felicity Lake, I have no desire to become a P.I. myself. My role is in the office, performing the admin duties that allow you to go out and fight the monsters without worrying about the paperwork. I've previously worked with three other P.I.s, all in Canada. My last posting was in Thompson, Manitoba. I requested a transfer to the States because my wife and I wanted to live somewhere a little bit warmer. I was expecting to be posted somewhere further south but here I am in Maine." His disappointment was evident in the grin he offered.

"Sorry that didn't work out for you," I said.

"I'm sure we'll grow to love it here. And you don't have to worry about me leaving anytime soon. Once I'm settled somewhere, I don't move on unless I have to."

"You left Manitoba to come here. Are you sure you aren't going to ask to be transferred somewhere further south?"

He looked a little sheepish. "Actually, I had to leave Manitoba."

"Oh? Why was that?"

"The P.I. I was working for got herself killed by a troll. It was quite tragic."

"You said you worked for three P.I.s previously. What happened to the other two?"

"They were also killed. After they died, the Society asked me to stay and work with their replacements but I felt it was time to move on. It's only a tragedy that will get me to move to a new posting, Mr Harbinger, so you needn't fear, I'll be here in Dearmont for as long as you need me. I won't be going anywhere unless...something terrible happens to you."

"That's very comforting," I said sarcastically.

"That came out all wrong. What I meant to

say was that I won't just abandon you like your previous assistant."

"Felicity isn't abandoning me, she got promoted," I told him.

"Yes, of course. That came out wrong too. Sorry. Maybe if you tell me what open cases we have at the moment, I can review them and get myself up to speed, eh?"

"We don't have any open cases at the moment. We're currently working on an issue that arose during one of our older cases."

"Oh? What might that be? Is there a file I can read?"

I indicated the computer on the desk. "You have access to the computer, right?"

He nodded. "Of course."

"Look up a case we handled regarding John DuMont and an artifact called the Box of Midnight. There should be some notes on there about the curse that befell Mallory. Familiarize yourself with the case and be at my house at noon. I assume you know my address?"

"Yes, I do. My wife and I will be moving into the house next door tomorrow."

"Oh. Yeah." I'd forgotten that as my new assistant, Carlton would also be my new neighbor.

"Be there at noon," I reminded him before leaving the office.

Mallory and I went back down the stairs and outside to the Land Rover.

When we were inside the car, she said, "He seems eager to please."

I started the engine and headed toward the grocery store. "Yeah, he does. There's just one thing that worries me."

"What's that?"

"When a P.I. gets a new assistant, it's standard procedure to contact the P.I.s who worked with the assistant in the past and ask them for a reference. I can't do that because everyone Carlton has ever worked with is dead."

5

Mallory and I got back home at eleven thirty with the groceries. It had finally stopped raining but the roads were slick with moisture.

A patrol car was parked on the street and Merlin and Amy were standing at Felicity's front door, talking to her. I parked the Land Rover outside my house and went around to the back of the vehicle to get the sacks of food Mallory and I had bought at the store.

Amy came over and said, "Need some help with that?"

I nodded. "Sure, thanks."

As she took a couple of sacks out of the Land Rover, she said, "Merlin asked me for the phone numbers of people he should invite to the party. I decided to call them myself. I hope that's okay. He isn't so good on a phone."

"Of course it's okay. I only asked Merlin to do it because he was with me at the time." I grabbed three sacks and opened the front door.

"It was all pretty sudden, huh? Must have been quite a shock for you. I know how invaluable Felicity has been." Amy asked as she stepped into the house and headed to the kitchen.

"Yeah," I said, following her. "I don't think it's really sunk in yet."

We dropped the sacks onto the counter and Mallory came in with a couple of cases of beer, which she placed next to the sacks.

"Are they going to send someone to replace her?" Amy asked.

I sighed, thinking of Carlton Carmichael. "They already have. He's at the office right now, familiarizing himself with the case involving the Box of Midnight and the curse."

She raised a quizzical eyebrow. "I can tell you're not too keen him. What's his name?"

"Carlton Carmichael."

"And why don't you like him?"

"I didn't say that. I've barely met the guy."

"The last three P.I.s he worked with are all dead," Mallory said.

Amy looked shocked. "Wow!"

"That isn't necessarily strange," I said. "Being a P.I. is dangerous. It's probably just Carlton's bad luck that everyone he worked with came to an untimely end." I paused while I tried to work out how to explain what I felt about Carlton's past record of misfortune. "I don't want his bad luck to rub off on me."

"You mean you don't want to be the fourth dead P.I. on his resumé?" she asked.

"Exactly. He seems to attract misfortune and that's the last thing I need."

"I didn't realize you were superstitious, Alec."

I shrugged. "Maybe a little. Sometimes it pays to err on the side of caution."

Amy nodded. "I guess I can't argue with that."

The three of us unpacked the snack food and loaded it onto plates, dishes, and bowls which we placed on the kitchen table along with the bottles of beer.

Felicity came into the room. She was wearing jeans and a black blouse and had obviously spent time on her hair and makeup. I looked down at my flannel shirt and T-shirt, which were still damp from the rain and sighed. I should have changed into something more appropriate for a party. I didn't want Felicity's memory of me to be of a scruffy guy in wet clothes with unkempt hair.

"Thank you for doing this," she said, smiling. "It makes me feel appreciated."

"You *are* appreciated," I told her. "I don't know

what I'd have done without you these past few months."

"Likewise," she said. "You've taught me so much about being a P.I."

"I'm not sure about that. I may have taught you what *not* to do."

She laughed lightly. "You know that isn't true."

Carlton Carmichael stuck his head around the door. "The policeman outside said I should come right in, I hope that's okay." His eyes found Felicity and he went to her, hand outstretched. "Miss Lake, congratulations on your new position within the Society. I'm Carlton Carmichael, your replacement."

"Oh." Felicity shook his hand, seemingly taken aback by Carlton's presence. I guessed that, like me, she hadn't expected her replacement to arrive so quickly. "Hello, Carlton, it's nice to meet you," she said, quickly recovering—at least outwardly—from her shock. "I'm sure you'll enjoy working with Alec and his team."

"I'm sure I will," he agreed. "And I must commend you on your case reports. I've read through many of them and they are quite impressive."

"Thanks," Felicity said. "Hopefully they'll bring you up to speed on what's going on around here. Are you hoping to become a P.I. yourself?"

"Oh, no, not at all. The office is my

battleground and the only thing I fight is the paperwork."

Merlin appeared at the kitchen door and announced, "The remaining two members of the Scooby Gang have arrived." With a flourish of his arms, he indicated Leon and Michael, who were standing next to him.

"Yeah, err, thanks for the introduction," Leon said. He went to Felicity and hugged her. "I'm so sorry you're leaving. I'm going to miss you but I'm happy for you too."

"Thank you, Leon," Felicity said, holding him tight.

"Congratulations on your new appointment, Miss," Michael said.

Felicity released Leon and hugged Michael. "Thank you."

"Maybe we should move into the living room," I said. "Everyone grab a beer and some food. The paper plates are over there."

Everyone moved toward the table and began filling their plates.

When we were all settled in the living room, Felicity, who had remained standing, said, "There are some things I need to tell you all regarding what you'll be facing when you lift the curse. I've researched the subject quite extensively, especially during the last few weeks, and now that I'm leaving, I need to pass on everything I've learned."

Everyone sat forward attentively.

"Rekhmire was the high priest of Heliopolis during the reign of Amenhotep the Third," Felicity began. "Amenhotep was the ninth Pharaoh of the Eighteenth Dynasty and ruled Egypt from approximately 1386 to 1349 BC. A sorceress named Tia was part of Amenhotep's court. She cast spells and enchantments and used her power of prophecy for Amenhotep. It seems that Rekhmire, the priest, became jealous of Tia's closeness to the Pharaoh."

She took a swallow of beer before continuing. "Eventually, Rekhmire's jealousy consumed him so much that he decided to destroy both the sorceress and the Pharaoh by using dark magic. A jubilee was held to celebrate 30 years of Amenhotep's rule and the festivities took place at the Pharaoh's summer palace in Western Thebes. At the hour of midnight, during the jubilee celebrations, Rekhmire murdered Tia and cut out her heart. He magically sealed her heart into a box of gold and silver that came to be known as the Box of Midnight."

I felt Mallory's body stiffen beside me on the sofa. I looked over at her. She was staring at the floor in front of her feet, taking long, slow breaths. Beads of sweat covered her face.

"Are you okay?" I whispered to her.

She turned to me and for a moment didn't seem to recognize me. Then she nodded. "It's just this story. I've seen Tia's murder played out in my head over and over and it gets to me every time."

That was understandable. Tia's spirit inhabited Mallory's body so it was possible that their emotions were intertwined in some way.

"Are you all right, Mallory?" Felicity asked, a concerned look on her face.

"Yeah, I'm fine," Mallory said. "Please, continue."

"Okay," Felicity said uncertainly. "Rekhmire also fashioned a staff with which he could channel magical power from the box and raise the dead. He raised an undead army and attempted to destroy Amenhotep. He failed. Amenhotep's soldiers were victorious in the battle that ensued and Rekhmire went into exile. At that point he disappears from the history books."

She cast a worried glance at Mallory, who still seemed to be going through an internal struggle to control her emotions.

Mallory noticed the pause and said, "Don't worry about me."

"My parents are Egyptologists," Felicity said, "While I was at their house, I discovered some references to the curse that was placed on the box of Midnight, the curse that states that anyone who destroys the heart inside the box will only have one year left to live. It's called the Heart Curse and there's a painting on the wall of Amenhotep's tomb that depicts Rekhmire creating the box. At least, that's what all the Egyptologists and historians have always believed. I think they're wrong and the painting shows something else entirely."

She paused to drink more beer. "The painting is believed to show a ritual known as the Sealing of the Heart. I found a description of the painting in a book called *Wonders of the Tombs,* written by a man named Charles Walpole in the 1930s. Walpole described the painting as showing a priest removing a heart from a person and placing it inside a magical box."

Felicity cast a quick glance at Mallory before continuing. "In my father's study, I found a photograph of the painting. It shows a man standing face to face with a mummy. On the floor between them is a box and the man is holding a heart. Walpole had mistakenly assumed this image showed the heart being removed from the mummy. But the Heart Curse requires a living heart and a living heart can't be taken from a mummy. So I believe the heart in the painting has been removed from the box and the man is about to place it inside the mummy. It's the reverse of what everyone thinks the painting shows but it's the only thing that makes sense."

She drained her beer bottle before adding, "I think the painting shows how to lift the curse. The heart has to be placed back into the mummified body of the person it came out of. In this case, that's Tia, the sorceress."

Mallory doubled over, clutched her stomach, and let out a low moan. Her hair fell over her face, obscuring it completely, but I guessed that there would be hieroglyphs pushing against the skin of her cheeks and forehead, the same as I'd seen when we were being questioned by the Shadow Watch agents in Bangor.

"I will have vengeance," Mallory whispered in a strained voice that was not her own. "Rekhmire must die for what he did to me."

"Mallory," I said, placing a hand gently on her shoulder. "Don't let Tia's emotions consume you."

She lifted her head to face me. As I'd suspected, her skin was raised in the shape of various hieroglyphs. The irises of her eyes—which were usually hazel in color—had turned black and melded with her pupils.

She shrugged my hand away, "Rekhmire must be destroyed."

"We're working on it," I told her.

"No," she said. "You are talking. Not killing. Not destroying."

"It isn't that simple. We have to find him first."

She let out a frustrated grunt and picked up a marker from the coffee table. Then she went to the wall and began drawing on it.

"I don't think you should be doing that," Carlton told her. "This house belongs to the Society of Shadows. You shouldn't vandalize Society property."

"Let her do what she has to do," I said. If my hunch was right, she was going to draw the same two pillars and hieroglyphs she'd scrawled on the wall of Mallory's hotel room. Maybe she'd explain what they meant too.

She drew the exact same thing she'd drawn on the hotel room wall and turned to face me, pointing at the symbols and the two pillars with her finger. "This is how we find him."

"What does it mean?"

Instead of answering, she stumbled forward in a faint. Felicity caught her and laid her down on the carpet.

Mallory's eyes flickered open. They were back to their normal color.

"Are you okay?" I asked.

She nodded, pushing herself up from the floor. "Tia takes over sometimes. I could feel her power rising every time Felicity mentioned Rekhmire's name. She's fuelled by her pure hatred for him."

"I just hope her hatred will help us when we come face to face with him," I said as she resumed her seat next to me on the sofa.

"What just happened?" Carlton asked.

"I'll explain later," I told him.

"Sorry for the interruption, Felicity," Mallory said.

Felicity smiled at her. "No problem. It wasn't your fault." She inspected the lotus pillars that were scrawled onto the wall and traced her fingers over some of the hieroglyphs.

"Do you know what it means?" I asked.

She shook her head. "I'd have to carry out some further research, which I obviously can't do now that I'm leaving." She turned to Carlton. "I'll leave this in your hands."

My new assistant nodded. "As you say, it will take some time to interpret the hieroglyphs."

"I can see from first glance that the name of the Egyptian god Khonsu is mentioned in there a few times," Felicity said.

Carlton nodded. "Yes, it is."

"Khonsu is the ancient Egyptian god of the moon," Felicity said, turning to address the room. "His name means "traveler" so perhaps this message and these pillars are part of a ritual that concerns traveling."

"Probably," Carlton agreed.

"The lotus designs on the pillars and these

specific symbols remind me of something I've seen before," Felicity said.

Carlton nodded knowingly. "Yes, me too. I've definitely seen them somewhere before."

Maybe my new assistant was trying to make a good first impression by appearing knowledgeable but the lack of substance behind what he was saying was having the opposite effect. He hadn't offered anything new to the conversation and was simply parroting Felicity's words.

"Getting back to my original train of thought," Felicity said. "You need to find Tia's mummy and place her heart into her body. I believe this will reverse the curse on Mallory. Be careful, though, because Rekhmire will keep the mummy close so when you find the mummy, you also find him and, according to everything I've read, he's very dangerous. He's working on a plan to raise an army of the dead and annihilate the world. He may have failed in that task thousands of years ago but he's going to try it again. All of the writings concerning him are apocalyptic in nature."

"We'll be careful," I assured her.

"Good," she said. "Well, that's all the information I have to pass on regarding the curse so let's eat and drink and enjoy ourselves."

The party got into full swing and soon

everyone was exchanging stories and jokes about past cases and experiences.

I watched Carlton Carmichael closely. He listened to the banter and joined in occasionally, trying to become a part of our close-knit group.

I wanted to give him the benefit of the doubt but my recent experience with the Society—when they'd sent two Shadow Agents to question me about my father—made me suspicious. Was he simply here to help or had he been handed some ulterior motive by the people who'd sent him here?

One thing was certain; I was going to be hitting the books tonight. Carlton's seeming lack of knowledge about the hieroglyphs on my wall meant I couldn't trust him to interpret Tia's message.

6

They came for Felicity at seven thirty.

I was sitting on the floor of my living room with half a dozen books about ancient Egyptian magic and architecture spread out in front of me when I heard the car coming through the rain, splashing along the water on the street.

Shrugging on my jacket, I went outside into the downpour. It was dark and a cold wind drove the rain into my face.

The car—a black Bentley—was parked outside Felicity's house, its headlights cutting through the night.

Felicity had said goodbye to everyone at the party but I couldn't just stay in my house while she stole into the night. That seemed wrong somehow.

She came out of the front door trailing a

suitcase behind her. In her other hand, she held a large black umbrella.

"Here, let me get that," I said, going to her.

"Thank you, Alec." She relinquished the luggage and held up the umbrella so that it was protecting both of us from the rain as we walked to the Bentley.

"I'm going to miss this place," she said with a sigh.

"And you'll be missed," I said. "But you have a great future ahead of you as a P.I. You'll be one of the best, I have no doubt about that."

She smiled. "I'll let you know how I get on."

The driver got out of the car and opened the trunk, taking the luggage from me without a word and stowing it before getting back into the car.

"Well, this is it," Felicity said.

"Text me when you land so I know you arrived safely."

"I will. Thank you, Alec. For everything." She leaned forward and we hugged awkwardly beneath the umbrella.

"Now you get back inside," she told me as she collapsed the umbrella and opened the rear car door. "This weather is awful. At least it will prepare me for the English rain." She got into the car and I closed the door for her.

The car slid away from the curb and into the night.

I stood on the sidewalk in the cold rain, watching the car until it turned at the end of the street and disappeared from view.

And that was that. Felicity was gone. Every time I thought about the fact that I wouldn't work with her again, a hollowness grew in my gut. But she couldn't have stayed here working as my assistant forever; she was destined for better things than that. I'd meant what I'd said about her being a damn good P.I. She was going to help a lot of people.

I turned away from the empty street and went back inside my house. After getting soaked in the rain, I decided to take a hot shower and get back to the books later. I wasn't exactly getting anywhere. It had been too long since I'd done my own research and I was rusty. Relying on Felicity too much in the past had dulled my skills.

When I got out of the shower and returned to the living room, wearing fresh, dry clothes, I heard a noise outside and peered through the window to check it out.

A large black unmarked truck was parked outside Felicity's house and a small army of men dressed in black sweaters, jeans, and watch caps were swarming back and forth from the house to the truck with boxes and crates.

The Society really didn't waste any time.

I hit the books and tried to ignore the noise outside. But as I tried to read an old Society text about temples dedicated to the god Khonsu, I couldn't concentrate on the words. I read the last two paragraphs again but my brain wasn't taking anything in. My thoughts kept wandering to the situation next door where all of Felicity's things were being taken away.

There was no point in trying to flog a dead horse so I closed the books and pushed them aside. I turned on the TV but couldn't concentrate on anything. Eventually, I just channel surfed until I found a rerun of Miami Vice and left that playing in the background as an accompaniment to my drifting thoughts.

My eyes eventually became drawn to the symbols on the walls that had been scrawled there by Tia, the sorceress. I stared at the image intently for a few minutes, as if by doing so I might be able to absorb the shapes into my mind and unlock their secrets through mere familiarity.

Yeah, that wasn't going to happen.

I went to the window again and looked out at the Society truck. It was already leaving, rolling toward the end of the street with Felicity's personal possessions inside. One of the guys in black had stayed behind. He got into the Mini and backed out of the driveway before following the truck into the rainy night.

And that was that. The house next door, which had been Felicity's home for the past few months, was now empty.

I went down to the basement, where my training area was set up. Sitting and staring at books all evening had made me edgy and I needed to expend some energy. I put my boxing gloves on and approached the heavy bag in a fighter's stance. A few jabs and a left hook took me into a workout that soon had me sweating and breathing hard.

The bag rattled on its chains with each punch. As my muscles warmed up, I increased the ferocity of my attacks, ducking and weaving to avoid hits from an imaginary opponent before following up with powerful hooks and lightning fast jabs.

I didn't stop until I was gasping for air and sweating so much I felt like I'd just stepped out of a shower.

But I still wasn't done.

I dragged one of the training dummies to the padded area in the center of the room and took a sword from the weapon rack. Utilizing various lines of attack, I struck the dummy from different angles before retreating quickly to practice my footwork.

After working on the dummy for almost an hour, I replaced the sword in the rack and stood with my hands on my hips while I caught my breath. Despite the intense workout I'd just had and the fact that my body ached, I still wanted more. But hitting inanimate objects wasn't doing it for me; I needed something that would fight back.

Since I'd killed the only monster I was aware of in the area—the ghoul at the Whispering Pines Cemetery—I didn't have many options for a flesh and blood opponent.

But maybe there was something else I could fight.

I eyed the cupboard on the wall.

Every time I'd used Excalibur, the sword had fought against my control, twisting in my grip and trying to guide my arm as if it were in charge of my body. I'd played around with the weapon a little in the past but I hadn't actually used it for long enough to know if I could take control of the damned thing or if it was too strong for me.

Time to find out.

I opened the cupboard door and peered inside. The sword hung on its peg expectantly. That's a weird way to describe a weapon but I could feel Excalibur's anticipation flowing out of the cupboard. For all I knew, the damned thing was alive; it certainly felt that way sometimes.

Wrapping my fingers around the red and gold thread that bound the handle, I lifted the weapon from the peg and hefted it in my hand as if testing its weight.

"Okay," I told it, "I'm going to attack that dummy but I'm going to pull my strike before I actually make contact. If you think you can force the blow to land, give it your best shot." The last time I'd used Excalibur to attack one of the training aids, the sword had chosen to decapitate the dummy despite the fact that I'd been aiming at the chest.

Taking the sword to the training area, I stood in front of the dummy and decided to attack the chest again and stop the momentum of the blade before it struck home. I'd be ready if Excalibur tried to change the line of my attack and strike the head or neck.

"Here we go," I said, stepping forward and swinging the blade at the dummy's chest area. The sword didn't fight me at all. I halted the strike mere inches from the surface of the dummy's chest, exactly as I'd planned.

I drew back and looked down at Excalibur in my hand. "You're not going to fight? You're just going to let me do what I want? I'm disappointed."

Attacking the dummy again, I aimed at the torso and pulled the strike. Again, the sword did nothing to fight me. It was just as inanimate as any of my other weapons.

Except I knew Excalibur wasn't like any other sword. It had a mind of its own.

So why was it playing dead?

I took a few more swings at the dummy, trying to coax Excalibur into life.

Nothing. Maybe the sword had submitted to me without a fight.

"You don't want to play ball?" I said. "Fine, I'll just put you back in the cupboard."

The sword began to vibrate in my hand and I felt powerful energy spread up my arm. It felt like my veins had been injected with electricity.

I laughed. Excalibur hadn't surrendered to me at all. In fact, it had been fighting me for power from the moment I'd taken it off the peg by refusing to follow the rules I'd set for our little game. I'd told it to fight me and it had refused. It had won by not participating.

The only leverage I seemed to have over the sword was that I could put it away. Once I'd threatened to put it back in the cupboard, it had ended its charade.

It obviously wanted to be in my hands. It was giving me some sort of energy but was it also drawing energy from me in some sort of exchange?

That was creepy. I had no intention of

entering into some sort of symbiotic relationship with a sword.

I thrust it into the cupboard and closed the door. My workout was done and I had no intention of hanging around in the basement any longer.

I ascended the steps and switched off the light. The basement was plunged into darkness.

As I closed the door, I was sure I heard the sword whispering to me from that darkness.

7

I woke up the next morning, checked the time on my alarm clock and groaned. It wasn't morning at all. It was almost midday. Last night's workout had wiped me out.

When I sat up in bed, my joints and muscles protested, sending waves of pain through my body. A headache loomed at the back of my skull. I hadn't drunk much alcohol yesterday had I? Because the symptoms I was experiencing felt like a hangover.

I'd only had a couple of beers so there was no way I was hung over.

Climbing gingerly out of bed, I padded to the bathroom and took a cold shower. Maybe that— and a couple of Tylenol—would clear the cobwebs in my head.

But almost an hour later, when I was standing

in the kitchen and drinking my second cup of coffee, I still felt like I'd gone ten rounds with a Peterbilt truck.

I went to the living room and sat on the sofa while I finished the cup of coffee. Outside, the street glistened wetly. The rain had stopped sometime during the night and the sun was shining in the dull gray sky but it didn't look like it was taking the edge off the Fall chill.

Maybe I'd caught a virus standing out in the cold rain last night.

Damn, I hadn't checked my phone for a message from Felicity and it was lying on my nightstand. That meant going back upstairs and enduring the throbbing in my head with every step.

I had to know that Felicity was okay so I was just going to have to take the discomfort that came with moving. I got up and warily took a few steps toward the stairs. Pain bloomed in my head like a dark flower and I reached a hand out to the sofa to steady myself.

When the throbbing had subsided enough that I felt I could move again, I let go of the sofa and stumbled forward like a child taking a hesitant first step.

The dark flower blossomed and my legs lost all strength. I hit the carpet with a thud.

Rolling over onto my back, I stared up at the

ceiling and tried to regain my composure. A cold sweat had broken out on my forehead and my breathing was shallow, making me feel light headed.

This was no virus that a shot of vitamins would cure. Something else was happening here.

Along with the pain in my head, there was now a deep throbbing in my right forearm. Maybe I'd twisted it when I'd fallen. I lifted it in front of my face to check for a bruise. What I saw was more than a mundane injury. Much more.

The veins in my hand, wrist, and forearm had turned dark blue, almost black. The darkness snaked up to my elbow, where it faded away.

Sitting up and leaning back against the sofa, I inspected my arm closely. The area that had been effected was the same place I'd felt the jolt of energy from Excalibur. Had the damned sword done this to me?

I needed to call Merlin. Maybe this was a side effect of using the sword that he'd forgotten to tell me about.

But I couldn't call him. My phone was upstairs and I was pretty sure I couldn't make it to the foot of the stairs, never mind ascend them and get to the bedroom.

I was just going to have to wait it out and hope I regained my strength.

I closed my eyes and rested my head against the sofa.

"Alec." The whispered voice slid into my mind like a hot knife slipping through butter.

I knew that voice. It was the voice of the sword.

"Go away," I groaned. I didn't have the time or energy for this crap.

"Alec." The voice was seductive, beckoning.

"Leave me alone."

"Alec." The sword was persistent.

"Get out of my head."

"Alec."

I should go down there and melt the damned thing in the furnace, turn it into a pair of candlesticks or something. Unfortunately, I didn't even have enough energy to move so melting down legendary swords was out of the question.

How long was I going to have to wait here until I got my strength back?

Would it ever come back?

Of course it would. All I needed was something to get me back on my feet.

"Alec."

The sword knew what I needed. Was it offering me more of what it had given me last night?

A jolt of that energy would feel good right now.

My eyes moved to the door that led down to the basement. I might not be able to go upstairs to get my phone but going downstairs would be easy, right? Gravity would do most of the work.

Leaning forward, I half-rolled, half-crawled to the door. Every muscle ached and every inch of progress was hard won. When I finally reached the door, I opened it and leaned against the wall while I regained my breath. Every beat of my heart made my head pound. I closed my eyes and waited for my heartbeat to slow down and for the throbbing to ease off a little.

Two torturous minutes passed before I could open my eyes again.

The stairs descended into darkness.

Excalibur whispered to me from down there. It wasn't saying my name anymore; the whispered words sounded like no language I'd heard before.

I leaned forward and I tumbled down into the darkness. When I hit the floor at the bottom of the stairs, the air was knocked out of my lungs and I struggled to catch my breath.

The whispering was louder down here. The strange words meant nothing to me but their meaning was clear; the sword was offering me a jolt of energy. This weakness would disappear. I'd be strong again.

Crawling across the padded training area floor in the dark, I could feel Excalibur's power. The air around me hummed. Green sparks flashed in the darkness.

I got to the cupboard on the wall and reached up for it. Just pulling open the door took a tremendous effort.

I reached inside and my hand touched the blade. The sharp steel cut into my palm but I didn't take my hand away. Energy flowed from the sword like molten electricity into my veins. I closed my eyes and accepted it. As it flooded through my body, I felt stronger than ever before. It hit my brain with a rush of euphoria that made me cry out.

Getting to my feet, I wrapped my bloody hand around the sword's handle and pulled it out of the cupboard. Excalibur and I were one. I strode into the training area and whirled the sword around my head, taking swings at imaginary opponents in the dark. The blade crackled and threw off green sparks as it sliced through the air.

With this weapon in my hand, I could destroy anyone or anything that stood in my way. The prospect of taking down the entire Midnight Cabal was no longer a flight of fancy; with

Excalibur in my hand, I could eradicate every last member of that hateful organization.

I continued to attack imaginary foes, pivoting on my feet and moving the sword in intricate, spark-laced patterns in the air in front of me. My movements, combined with the delicate arcs of the blade, became a dance that fused man and weapon.

When it was over, I was covered in a sheen of sweat and breathing hard.

I felt amazing.

Excalibur's blade glowed dimly in my hand, as if reflecting light from somewhere even though the basement was pitch black.

I didn't want to let the sword go but I had things to do. Regretfully, I placed it back into the cupboard and went back upstairs, taking the steps two at a time.

I needed to get to the office. Without Felicity to open up, everything fell to me and it was already the afternoon.

Bounding upstairs, I grabbed my phone and checked it. There was a text message from Felicity.

Landed in London. Everything fine. Hope all goes well with your new assistant.

At least I knew she was okay. I replied with a message wishing her well in her new job.

I went back downstairs, grabbed a handful of

the leatherbound Egyptian magical texts from the floor, and left the house. I threw the books into the backseat of the Land Rover and turned to take a look at Felicity's empty house.

Except it wasn't empty. A pair of matching white Honda Civics sat on the driveway.

Surely Carlton hadn't moved in already. Felicity had only left a few hours ago.

As I looked at the house, frowning, the front door opened and Carlton came out. With a smile, he gave me a short wave and said, "Hey, neighbor."

8

When I got to the office, I put the Egyptian books on my desk and booted up the computer. Without Felicity fussing about the place—or just knowing she was in the next room—the office was a lonely place. Too quiet. Too empty.

I rolled my chair over to the window and looked out at Main Street. As usual, the good folk of Dearmont were going about their daily business and the street was bustling with people and cars. I groaned when I saw Carlton Carmichael approaching the building.

Maybe I was being hard on the guy. He deserved a chance to fit into the team. It wasn't his fault he was following in Felicity's footsteps.

He opened the door and came up the stairs. He poked his head into the office. "Hi, Boss.

Sorry I'm late. We spent the morning moving into our new home."

"Yeah, I noticed. That was pretty quick. Felicity only left last night."

"I know, right? I guess the Society wanted us *in situ* as quickly as possible. What are you gonna do?"

"Yeah," I repeated. "What are you gonna do? Now that you're here, you can check the answering machine and see if we have any new cases."

"Okay, Boss." He turned away from my door and went into his office.

"And there's no need to call me Boss," I shouted after him. "Alec will do just fine."

I returned to the computer and scanned the local news sites, looking for anything that might indicate preternatural activity in the area. The first article I found was a follow up on the story about Linda Whittington's missing body. The headline read, *More Trouble at Local Cemetery*.

According to the story, a group of teenagers had been fooling around in the Whispering Pines Cemetery last night when a "hideous creature" had appeared from behind one of the tombstones and chased them all the way to their cars. The teenagers had raced away and gone to the police. An officer had checked out the cemetery and found a hole in the ground which seemed to be some sort of tunnel. The policed planned to carry out a more in-depth investigation of the tunnels today.

I let out a sigh of frustration. I should have checked for more ghouls in those tunnels when I was there a couple of nights ago. It looked like there was a nest at Whispering Pines after all. And since I'd killed one of their number, the remaining ghouls were going to be pissed.

I had to get over there before the police poked their noses into those tunnels and got them bit off.

The only problem I could see was that I might be spotted if I went to the cemetery in broad daylight. A sword-wielding guy climbing down into a hole among the graves might raise a few eyebrows. But I couldn't risk the police getting there before me. If they stumbled upon a nest of ghouls, there would be casualties.

Not on my watch.

I went out into the hall and glanced into Carlton's office. He was making coffee.

"Did you check the machine?" I asked.

"Yeah, no messages. We might have a quiet day."

"There's still work to be done. I have to go out. While I'm gone, take a look through the books on my desk and see what you can find out about those pillars, the god Khonsu, anything that will help us get to Tia's mummy."

He nodded eagerly. "Will do."

I left the building and almost collided with Leon, who was coming in the door as I was going out.

"Hey. Alec, you going somewhere?"

"Yeah, I need to deal with a problem."

"Oh, cool, because I was in the area and I was wondering if you needed any—"

"You can come with me, Leon. I'd appreciate the help."

His face broke into a grin. "Awesome. So what are we doing?"

"Pest control." I told him about the ghouls at Whispering Pines as we walked to the Land Rover.

As we got into the car, he said, "You got weapons?"

I nodded. "In the back. Swords and daggers."

He sat back in his seat and nodded. "Excellent. Anything new regarding Mallory's case?"

I started the Land Rover and joined the traffic on Main Street. "Nothing yet. I've been looking through the books but I can't find anything about pillars like the ones Tia drew on my wall. I told Carlton to take a look. Maybe he'll find something I missed."

"I doubt that," Leon said. "He doesn't seem to have anything like Felicity's level of expertise."

"We have to give him a chance to prove himself."

"I guess so."

I stopped at the hardware store, where I purchased four large plastic bottles of lye. I had no idea how many ghouls we might encounter and I wanted to make sure I had enough of the chemical to destroy everything. After stowing the bottles in the back of the Land Rover, I got onto the highway and headed for the cemetery.

We rode in silence for a while, and then Leon said, "Do you think it's odd how quickly Carlton arrived?"

I'd been thinking exactly the same thing, especially since Carlton moved next door to me so fast but I simply said, "What do you mean?" I valued Leon's opinion and I wanted to hear his theory about my new assistant before I offered my own.

"Felicity gets snatched away by the Society and this guy is already waiting in the wings to replace her," he said. "It all happened so fast. I guess what I'm trying to say is: has Felicity been taken away because there's a new job for her or because the Society wants Carlton here instead of her?"

"You think he's a spy?" The same thought had

crossed my mind. When Felicity had first come to work for me, I'd accused her of being a spy and I hadn't been wrong; she'd been sent by my father to keep an eye on me. Had Carlton been sent by the Society to carry out a similar task?

"Maybe," Leon said. "Especially after you had those Shadow Watch agents all up in your business. Seems to me the Society thinks you know something about that Codex thing those guys were after."

"The Melandra Codex," I said. I'd been questioned about it by Honoka Chan and Todd Benson, two agents from the Shadow Watch. They seemed to think I knew the location of the Codex because my father might have told me where he'd hidden it. That was a joke; my dad hardly told me anything. I was the last person he'd tell about the location of a Codex he'd allegedly stolen from the Society.

"Yeah, Melandra Codex," Leon said. "Those Shadow Watch agents failed to get any info out of you, so what if the Society is trying something more subtle, like sending Carlton here to find out what you know?"

"It's possible," I said. "But if that's why Carlton is here, the Society has wasted its time. I have no idea what the Melandra Codex is or where it's hidden. I don't even know if my father ever had the Codex, as the

Society seems to believe. So Carlton can snoop around all he wants, he won't find anything."

"Nothing to worry about, then," Leon said.

"Nothing to worry about," I repeated.

We reached Whispering Pines Cemetery and my heart sank when I saw a patrol car in the parking lot.

Leon pointed at the car. "Looks like they beat us to it."

"That isn't good." I parked next to the patrol car and got out. "If they go into those tunnels unprepared, it won't end well for them."

"And who goes into a tunnel prepared to meet ghouls?" Leon slid out of the Land Rover and joined me at the tailgate. "They probably think those kids were pranking them. There's no way they believe there's a monster living at the cemetery."

"Exactly," I said, opening the tailgate and pulling back the blanket that covered the weapons. "Let's just hope they didn't go into the tunnels yet." I indicated the weapons. "The tunnels are too cramped for swords so we have to use daggers."

Leon chose one and balanced it in his hand. He made a few jabbing and slicing motions in the air, reminding me of my encounter with Excalibur earlier. The energy I'd received from the sword had dissipated slightly but I was still buzzing.

I grabbed a dagger and a flashlight and between us, we carried the bottles of lye.

We entered the cemetery and walked among the tombstones, looking for the hole the news site had mentioned.

"Over there," Leon said, pointing toward the far end of the cemetery. "Something's moving."

I squinted against the cold sun and saw what he was referring to. A low, dark was shape moving among the gravestones.

We sprinted along the path toward it and as we got closer, the shape became clearer. A blond-haired male police officer was crawling along the ground. He looked up at us and waved weakly. He was covered in dirt and blood. "Get out of here," he said. "There's something back there. Something dangerous."

The path he'd taken was clearly marked out by a trail of blood on the grass.

"I'll call an ambulance," I said.

"Already done. An ambulance and backup are on the way." He pointed vaguely in the direction of the blood trail. "My partner is back there. I think it got him. You have to leave."

"We're here to help," Leon told him.

"You can't help. Not against that thing. We need to wait for backup."

"How badly injured are you?" I asked, dropping the lye bottles and crouching beside him. The front of his uniform was stained with dark blood.

"It looks worse than it is," he said. "Damn thing clawed me in the stomach. I'm pretty sure it didn't hit anything vital but I'm losing blood."

"You need to stop crawling," I said. "Leon, help me get him into a sitting position." We carefully lifted the officer and sat him against the nearest tombstone.

"The ambulance should be here soon," I said. "Here, take this and keep it pressed against the wound." I took off my shirt and handed it to him.

"Thanks," he said, balling the shirt up and pressing it against his stomach. "If I pass out before backup gets here, tell them Dave Hooper is in the tunnel over there. Make sure they go in with their weapons ready."

"There's no time for that," I said. "We're going to help Dave. Wait here."

He shook his head weakly. "No, you can't go in there. There's something in those tunnels that isn't human."

"We know," Leon said, showing the police officer his dagger. "We're here to deal with it."

"With a knife?" He looked incredulous. "You can't go down there with a knife. That thing has claws like scythes.

"Don't worry about it," I said. "Just wait for that ambulance."

We left him leaning on the tombstone and followed the blood trail to a hole that angled into the ground.

"Looks like a tight squeeze," Leon said.

I shone the flashlight beam into the hole. It was narrower than the tunnels that made up the subterranean maze below and looked as if it had been made by the ghoul digging its way to the surface like a mole. "The main tunnels are larger," I told Leon. "This is just our way in."

He sighed. "Looks like I'm going to ruin a perfectly good set of clothing." He threw his bottles of lye into the hole, took the flashlight from me, and crawled in headfirst.

I followed close behind, crawling through the dirt until the narrow hole joined one of the main tunnels below. Once we were in the larger tunnel, I shook the dirt out of my hair and looked in both directions.

"It stinks down here," Leon said, wrinkling his nose. "Like rotting flesh."

"Yeah, that's what ghouls smell like."

"Which way?" Leon whispered.

The blue glow from our daggers illuminated the area around us but there were no clues to tell us where the ghoul and the other police officer might be.

"Let's go this way," I suggested, pointing north. "We'll leave the lye here. If we get into a fight, it'll slow us down. Here, it will act as a marker for the exit."

Leon nodded. "Good idea."

We crawled north along the tunnel. The foul smell in the air became stronger. A scream came from somewhere up ahead, confirming that we were heading in the right direction.

The tunnel bent to the left and as we rounded the corner, I saw a ghoul ahead of us, dragging a uniformed police officer into the darkness. Dave Hooper was screaming at the top of his lungs and struggling against the creature but it had its talons buried into his shoulders.

Hooper saw us and his eyes went wide. "Help! You've got to help me!"

The ghoul paused, seemingly weighing up its chances against Leon and me. Its beady eyes flicked between us and the glowing daggers we held in our hands. It must have decided it was better to live another day. It released Hooper and fled into the darkness.

Leon and I rushed forward as fast as we could in the cramped tunnel. Hooper was breathing hard and fast, his eyes staring at the tunnel wall.

"He's going into shock," I said to Leon. "See if you can get him back to the surface."

Leon nodded and began talking to the police

officer, trying to coax him back to the tunnel we'd used to enter the ghoul's lair.

Leaving them, I moved forward to chase down the creature I should have killed when I'd killed its mate. If I'd done a more thorough job, there wouldn't be two wounded police officers here right now. I shouldn't have assumed that the creature I'd encountered was the only one of its kind at Whispering Pines.

I held the dagger in front of me to light my way through the darkness. I couldn't see the ghoul. The damned things moved fast.

The tunnel twisted to the right and then opened up into a roughly square area that had a ceiling high enough that I could stand up. The smell of rotting flesh was overpowering. I quickly removed my T-shirt and wrapped it around my nose and mouth in an attempt to filter out the disgusting stench.

The blue dagger light revealed bones on the floor. As I moved deeper into the area, more bones appeared, forming a pile in one corner of the room. Some of the bones were picked clean while others still had pieces of flesh attached.

This had to be the nest.

But there was no sign of the ghoul.

I held the dagger close to the pile of bones to see if the creature was hiding under there, waiting to pounce at me. It wasn't. I checked the walls for exits or signs that the ghoul had tunneled its way out of here. The only tunnel that led from the nest was the one I'd used to enter. The creature had definitely not gone that way.

I angled the dagger up to check the ceiling. The ghoul was there, clinging to the dirt ceiling with its huge talons. It shrieked at me and dropped, spreading its fingers and slashing at me.

I wheeled away but my left shoulder lit up with searing pain as one of the claws caught me and ripped into my flesh. In the blue glow from my dagger, the blood that slicked my arm looked black. I was going to have to get to the surface soon; I had no idea how deep that cut went and if I passed out down here from loss of blood, I was as good as dead.

The ghoul had landed near the pile of bones. It coiled its body like an eager serpent and then used its powerful legs to launch itself at me.

I held the dagger out in front of me, hoping the creature would impale itself. I should have known I'd never be that lucky. The ghoul grabbed my wrist in its powerful shovel-like hand and held my blade out of the way while the trajectory and velocity of the leap brought its snout close to my face. It snapped at me.

I turned my head away just in time to avoid losing my nose and brought my knee up into the creature's stomach as hard as I could. It howled and loosened its grip on my hand enough that I could stab at its neck.

The dagger sank into its flesh and the ghoul jumped back, snarling and drooling. Blood oozed from a wound below its jaw but it didn't look like I'd managed to pierce anything important, like an artery. The creature's beady eyes were full of a hateful fire and it didn't look like it was going to perish from the wound anytime soon.

I wasn't fairing so well. My left arm was slick with blood and I felt light-headed. If I didn't get out of here soon and receive medical attention, I probably wasn't going to see tomorrow.

The ghoul sprang at me, roaring, probably sensing my weakness and going for a quick, easy kill.

If it thought I was going down easy, it was wrong. I dodged the attack and summoned enough strength to plunge the dagger into the creature's back as it passed me. Once the blade was in, I used both hands to draw it along the flesh by the ghoul's spine.

The creature landed in the dirt on its stomach, howling in pain. I dropped to my knees and buried the dagger in the back of its head, killing it.

When I was sure it was dead, I got to my feet, removed the T-shirt from my face and tied it tightly around my wound before stumbling out of the nest and along the tunnel. The darkness disorientated me and the blue light from the dagger seemed too dim to see by now. I needed to get out of here. I needed daylight.

When I saw the bottles of lye, I breathed a sigh of relief. It would be good to taste fresh air again after breathing the fetid, foul soup that passed for air down here.

I angled my body into the exit tunnel and crawled to the surface, sucking in a lungful of sweet, cold, Fall air when I finally emerged into the daylight. Gingerly, I lifted the tee from my shoulder and inspected the wound. It was still bleeding but it didn't look too deep.

Leon came running over to me. "Alec, are you okay? What happened?"

"It's dead," I told him. "That's all that matters. How are the officers?"

"The ambulance took them to the hospital. Come on, I'll drive you there."

I shook my head. "No hospital. I'll be okay."

"Dude, your arm—"

"It's okay. Just get me home and I'll sort it out there."

"If you're sure, man."

"Yeah, I'm sure. But before we leave, you have to do one more thing."

"Name it."

"You need to go back into the tunnel and

cover the ghoul's body with lye. And make sure there aren't any more in there."

He looked at the hole and nodded. "Okay. Wait here, I'll be back soon."

"I'm not going anywhere." I leaned against a tombstone and closed my eyes. Leon was still hanging around so I opened them again. He was taking off his shirt.

"What are you doing?"

He crouched next to me and put the shirt around my shoulders. "Here, you need to stay warm."

"Thanks," I mumbled. Exhaustion pressed on me like a weighted blanket. I watched as Leon went to the hole in the ground but then the world went blurry.

I slipped into the black hole of unconsciousness.

9

When I woke up, I was lying in the backseat of the Land Rover. Leon was driving. I sat up and leaned against the door, watching the world rush past the window for a moment while my head cleared.

It was raining. The windshield wipers whirred as they traveled across the glass. We were moving fast along the wet road. Water sprayed from beneath the tires and splashed against the car.

"Hey, you're awake," Leon said, eyeing me in the rearview mirror. "I was gonna take you to the hospital."

"I'm fine," I said. "Take me home, Leon. Please." My shoulder ached but at least the bleeding had almost stopped.

"You sure? You probably need stitches."

"I'm sure," I said. I wanted to clean and inspect the wound myself. If I thought I needed stitches after that, then I'd go to the hospital.

"You really should take care of yourself," Leon said. "Those two cops went to the hospital without any argument."

"Yeah, well they deserve to get the best care."

"So do you, man."

Did I? If it wasn't for me, those two officers wouldn't be in the hospital right now. They'd probably be at home with their families.

I'd let myself be distracted by Felicity's call and I hadn't checked for more ghouls. That was on me. The wound in my shoulder was the price I'd had to pay for being careless and I was going to let it heal in its own time. The scar that would eventually take its place would be a constant reminder that I had to be more vigilant.

"You sure you're okay?" Leon asked, watching me closely in the rearview.

"I'm sure."

When we got to my house, Leon parked the Land Rover on the driveway and helped me inside. I felt weary and I wasn't sure if that was due to a loss of blood or because the ghoul had given me an ass-kicking before I'd finally killed it.

Leon went to the bathroom to get medical supplies and I sank onto the sofa. I removed the

T-shirt from the wound. The blood-encrusted cut ran in a dead straight line down my shoulder, cutting through one of my magical protection tattoos. It didn't look deep enough to require stitches but the skin on either side of the wound had turned a sickly green color.

That wasn't right. I touched the green flesh gently with the tip of my finger. I had no feeling there.

"Shit."

"What's wrong?" Leon asked, coming into the room with the First Aid kit.

"I'm not sure. You see that green tinge around the wound?"

He inspected it closely. "Yeah, what the hell is that?"

This was the moment I would usually call Felicity and she'd tell me some little-known fact about ghoul scratches and tell me what to do to cure it.

Maybe Carlton would know something useful. It was probably a long shot but I had to try. The green color seemed to be spreading across my shoulder.

I called the office. Carlton picked up on the second ring. "Harbinger P.I. Carlton Carmichael speaking, how may I help you?"

"Carlton, it's me."

"Hi, Alec."

"Listen, what do you know about ghouls?"

"Ghouls? Well, I'll have to think back to the lessons of my academy days. I've never actually seen one in the flesh. What do you want to know?"

"Do they have a poisonous scratch or bite?"

"Hmm, I'm not sure. I can look it up if you like."

My shoulder was beginning to feel numb. "Yes, please."

"Okay, hold on a second." I heard him typing on his keyboard. "There doesn't seem to be much information here. Wait, here it is. Yes, the bite or scratch of a ghoul contains a poison that causes necrosis in the victim's tissue which eventually leads to death."

"Is there a cure?"

There was a pause and then he said, "It doesn't mention a cure. It wouldn't be a good idea to be scratched by one of those guys, eh?"

I hung up. Leon was on his phone. When he saw that I'd finished with Carlton, he hung up.

"It's bad news," I said. "The wound is going to turn necrotic and there's no cure listed in the Society database. Those two police officers are going to die because of me."

He frowned. "What do you mean because of you? We saved their asses."

"We saved them from a quick death and cursed them to a slow one."

"Not necessarily. While you were on the phone to Carlton, I called Merlin."

"Merlin?"

"Yeah, Merlin. If there's a cure, he'll probably know what it is. He was a druid, wasn't he? At least, that's what the stories say. Anyway, when I told him you'd been scratched by a ghoul, he sounded confident that he knew what to do."

I sat back on the sofa and looked up at the ceiling. "He always sounds confident, even when he has no idea what he's talking about."

"Well there isn't any other option. I could see you weren't getting anywhere with Carlton so I thought Merlin would be your best chance."

"Thanks," I said.

Half an hour, a knock sounded on the door and Leon answered it. Merlin pushed past him and carried a cardboard box of plants into the kitchen. Leon looked into the box and quickly drew his head back, his face screwed up in an expression of disgust.

"Dude, that smells like horse shit!"

"Among other things," Merlin said. "Now, I'll need a large pot in which to mix the ingredients and a stove to heat them up." He started rummaging through the kitchen cupboards.

Leon came back into the living room,

followed by the smell of whatever Merlin had in that box. "I'll open the windows," he said.

I nodded. "Good idea."

We sat in silence while Merlin heated a pot of God-knew-what on the stove. The smell was even worse now. Merlin, humming--a tune that was either a spell or a ditty he'd heard back in the Middle Ages--seemed oblivious to it.

When he was done, he brought the foul-smelling concoction into the living room in a bowl. In his other hand, he held a wooden spoon. "This poultice should have you back to normal in no time, Alec."

Siting on the coffee table, he spooned liberal amounts of the goopy stuff onto my shoulder. It didn't sting or even feel warm because by now, my shoulder was completely dead. I could smell the stuff though and turned my head away in an attempt to lessen the foul odor's assault on my senses. It didn't work.

"Don't use all of it," I told Merlin. "You need to use it on two police officers in the hospital as well as me."

"There's plenty to go round," he said cheerfully. "You're lucky I remember my druidical training. Otherwise, you'd be dead by morning. A ghoul's poison is no laughing matter."

"No one's laughing," Leon said.

Merlin sat back and inspected his handiwork.

"That should draw the poison out in no time. Once it dries and you feel all right again, just wash it away."

"Thanks," I said.

"I'll just use a quick spell to check you over." He held his hand over me and a dark blue glow emanated from them. Merlin closed his eyes and smiled. "Ah, yes, the poultice is working already. Good. good." Then his expression changed. His brows knitted together and his smile disappeared as his lips pursed. "What's this?" he muttered so quietly that he might be saying it to himself.

His eyes snapped open and he looked at me intently as he lowered his hands. The glow emanating from them dissipated. "You didn't tell me you were enchanted, Alec."

"I'm not," I told him.

"There's an enchantment inside you."

"Oh, that. I don't know what it is. Something happened to me when I was younger."

My childhood memory of lying in a cave surrounded by witches while my father watched from the shadows resurfaced. I pushed it away.

Merlin, still frowning, shook his head. "Whatever it is, I don't like it."

"Yeah, well I'm not exactly thrilled about it myself but I have to live with it."

He got up and collected his things from the kitchen. His usually ebullient mood was gone.

"I'll go to the hospital and see to those police officers," he said solemnly. Without another word, he left.

"What's eating him?" Leon asked.

"I have no idea." I tested my shoulder by poking it with my finger. I actually felt something. "At least this poultice seems to be working."

"Good," Leon said. "Could I borrow a shirt?"

His own shirt, the one he'd put around me in the cemetery was covered with blood.

"Of course. Take anything you want from my closet."

"Thanks, man." He went upstairs to the bedroom.

I wondered why Merlin had gotten so spooked. I wouldn't have thought a powerful wizard like him would be scared off by any sort of magic or enchantment. But when he'd left, there had been a look of fear in his eyes.

Trying to work Merlin out wasn't going to get me anywhere and besides, I should probably hit the books again. We still didn't have any leads regarding the location of Tia's mummy and I didn't hold any hope that Carlton would have discovered something. In fact, I regretted leaving the books with him at all because now I only had a handful of texts here to research.

I called Carlton at the office again. He'd

probably be leaving soon and I wanted to make sure he brought the books with him.

There was no answer.

Great. That meant he'd already left. Had he even cracked any of the books open? I'd know soon enough when he arrived home.

Leon came back downstairs wearing one of my red flannels.

"How are you getting on with the Midnight Cabal stuff?" I asked him. A couple of weeks ago, we'd purloined a laptop and a cache of electronic storage devices from a Cabal yacht. Leon, who was a computer genius, was trying to crack the coded material open.

"They have some powerful security measures," he told me. "I'll get past them but it'll take some time."

"Would you like to try something a little different?" I indicated the half-dozen Egyptian books scattered on the floor.

"Sure, anything to help Mallory."

"I'll order pizza and we can have a few beers while we work."

"Sounds good to me." He grabbed one of the books and settled into the easy chair.

I heard a car outside and went to the window to see if it was Carlton. It was. He parked his white Honda Civic on his driveway and got out of it in a hurry. Instead of going into his house, he ran over to my front door and knocked urgently.

"Come in, Carlton," I shouted to him.

He came through the door in a rush, breathing hard. He was wet from the rain that was still pouring down but there was a smile on his face. "I did it!" he said breathlessly. "I found the pillars!"

"Are you sure?" I asked.

"I was leafing through one of the books and there was a diagram of the pillars exactly like that." He pointed at the pictures of the pillars on my wall. "I know where they are."

"Where?"

"Egypt."

"Yeah, we kinda guessed that already."

"No, I know the precise location. It's all in the book."

I led him to the sofa and sat him down. "Okay, so where are the pillars."

"They're in a secret underground room."

"You said you knew the precise location."

He nodded. "The room is under the Sphinx!"

10

Felicity touched the frosted glass on the door and traced her fingers over the outline of the letters stenciled there.

Lake, P.I.

She'd done it. She'd achieved her dream of becoming a P.I. and her name on this door was proof of that. Her office wasn't exactly in the nicest part of Manchester but she didn't care. It was a perfect place to begin her career as a preternatural investigator.

She placed the key into the lock and opened the door. As it swung inward, stale air that smelled of mold and damp wafted out of the building. A set of wooden steps led up to the office. Felicity entered and ascended the creaking stairs to a landing whose floor was covered with old linoleum that had seen better days.

Unlike Alec's office, there was no room for an assistant. The Society had told Felicity in London that she wouldn't be getting an assistant and was expected to do her own paperwork. She was disappointed about that. Not because of the paperwork—she was used to that—but because it would have been nice to have someone around to talk to.

The landing had two doors. One led to a grimy bathroom, the other to a small room which was to serve as the office. There was a desk and chair in here, along with a telephone and an answering machine but that was all.

The Society seemed to have spared every expense. At least the house they'd provided Felicity with—which was a half hour drive away —was better appointed and furnished.

She opened the window to let the damp smell out and some fresh air in. While she was at the window, she took in the view of Manchester. Dark gray clouds hung over the city and heavy rainfall seemed imminent.

Turning back to the room, she noticed a red light flashing on the answering machine. She pressed the button to play the message.

A young woman's voice filled the room. "*Hello, my name is Jessica Baker and I've got a problem I think you can help me with. Please call me back when you can.*" She left a number and then the message ended.

Sitting on the edge of the desk, Felicity used the office phone to ring the number. Her first case. Would it be something simple or a complicated, deadly case that would test her resolve as a new P.I.? She really didn't mind which it was; it was a case and that was all that mattered.

The same voice that had been on the machine answered the phone. "Hello?"

"Hello, is this Jessica Baker?"

"Yes, who's this?"

"My name is Felicity Lake. You left a message for me to call you. I'm a P.I."

"Oh. I left that message a couple of days ago but then the office closed down. I didn't think anyone would call me back."

"I've taken over the business now," Felicity said, wondering what had happened to her predecessor. "So I'd like to help you if I can."

"That's great. Thank you."

"Would you like to come to the office and tell me how I can help?" She looked around the sparse space. She was going to have to get another chair from somewhere so her clients could sit down.

"Would you be able to come to my house? My

husband's taken the car to work and I don't fancy getting the bus."

"Of course," Felicity said, relieved her office would escape the scrutiny of a prospective client. She could hardly pass it off as shabby chic; the place was just dirty. Where was all the furniture that must have been here before?

"Shall we say one o' clock this afternoon?" she said into the phone.

"Yeah, that's great." Jessica gave her the address and then hung up.

Rain began to tap on the windows. Felicity went over to the window and looked out. The city looked somber beneath the gray sky.

She had a lot to do before she went to Jessica Baker's house. She had an appointment with a Society tattoo artist this morning. Like all P.I.s, she was required to have a number of protective magical symbols tattooed into her skin. These would prevent anyone from finding or tracking her by magical means and also offered some protection against certain spells and magical environments.

She'd never had a tattoo and didn't know what to expect. It couldn't be too bad; every Preternatural Investigator had them. Having the tattoos would be the final stage of her journey to becoming a P.I; an indelible confirmation of her role.

As she turned away from the window, a vehicle on the street below caught her eye. A black van parked across the street. Something about it unnerved her.

"Don't be silly," she told herself. "It probably belongs to someone who lives around here."

She knew that, logically, there was no reason to fear the van; it was probably parked there every day. But something inside her—something illogical but nonetheless real—made her feel anxious when she looked at the vehicle.

Checking her watch, she realized that if she didn't leave soon, she'd miss her appointment. There was no point standing in this smelly office looking at vans on the street when she had places to be. She went downstairs and out into the rain, locking the office door behind her. After taking another proud look at her name on the door, she hurried to the Ford Focus the Society had loaned her until her Mini arrived.

As she got in, she checked the rearview mirror and saw the black van again. Its windows were tinted so she couldn't see if there was anyone inside.

Telling herself to ignore the uneasiness she felt because it had no sound basis, she started the Focus and pulled away from the curb.

The heavy rain had slowed the traffic. Felicity punched the address she'd been given into the car's SatNav system and concentrated on getting across town. She suspected that her destination— a place called Mysterium Ink—was a regular tattoo studio that the Society ran as a front. It probably served ordinary members of the public and P.I.s alike. The non-Society clientele would have no idea that some of the customers being inked there were members of a secret organization being marked with tattoos that had a practical purpose.

She wondered how Alec and the others were getting on with the search for Tia's mummy. She'd considered ringing Alec last night but had ultimately decided against it. She wanted to get settled into her new life first so she could share it with him. Maybe after she'd worked the Jessica Baker case she'd have something to share.

If there was even a case there at all. She couldn't count the number of people who had sought Alec's help when they didn't need a P.I. at all. Some of them needed a private investigator rather than a paranormal investigator. Others were victims of an overactive imagination rather than a preternatural threat. Hopefully, Jessica Baker had a genuine problem which Felicity could solve.

She arrived at Mysterium Ink forty-five minutes later and parked in the customer car park at the rear. After hurrying from the car to the shop door, she pushed through into the warmth. Unlike the office Felicity had just left, Mysterium Ink was spotless. Gleaming white tiles covered the walls, which were adorned with framed pictures of tattoo designs. The air smelled faintly of antiseptic and there was a constant buzzing sound of tattoo guns.

Two clients sat in reclining leather chairs; a young man having a skull tattooed on his shoulder and an older woman who was having a red rose colored in on her ankle.

The girl at the front desk looked up at Felicity and said, "Hi, can I help you?"

"I have an appointment," Felicity said. "Felicity Lake."

The girl consulted a hardbound notebook in front of her and nodded. "Ah, yes. Your appointment is with Deb. I'll tell her you're here if you'd like to take a seat." She gestured to a row of plastic chairs by the window.

No sooner was Felicity seated than a short-haired woman in a black T-shirt and blue jeans came over. "Hey, Felicity. I'm Deb. Come with me and we'll get you sorted."

Felicity stood and smiled. Before following Deb, she took a last look at the rain swept street beyond the window.

What she saw made her heart skip a beat.

Parked across the street, its tinted windows staring at her like spider eyes, was the black van.

11

"What do you mean it's under the Sphinx?" I asked Carlton.

"Let me get the book and I'll show you." He went outside and ran back to his car.

"Do you think he's actually found something useful?" Leon asked, looking up from the book he'd been studying.

I shrugged. "I don't know. He seems pretty confident."

Carlton came back with a book tucked under his arm. He placed it on the coffee table and opened it to a page he'd marked with a scrap of paper. "Look at that," he said, pointing to an illustration on the page.

I looked at the illustration in the book and compared it to the drawing Tia had made on my wall. They were identical.

Leon studied the two drawings and let out a low whistle. "You found it, Carlton, old boy. Now, what were you saying about the Sphinx?"

"It says it right here," Carlton said, pointing to a line of Coptic characters on the page. "The Pillars of Khonsu reside beneath the human-lion guardian. A prayer that cannot be spoken in the day or night will open the gate."

"What the hell does that mean?" Leon asked, frowning. "A prayer that cannot be spoken in the day or night?"

"We can find that out later," Carlton said. "The point is, I found the pillars. They're under the Sphinx."

"They're not under the Sphinx," I told him.

He looked taken aback. His face flushed and his eyes narrowed. "What do you mean they aren't there? Look, it says it right here. The human-lion guardian. If that isn't the Sphinx then what does it mean, eh?"

"I agree it sounds like the Sphinx but it can't be. In 1998, an excavation was carried out beneath the Sphinx. There are some natural caverns and man-made tunnels and rooms down there but there are no pillars. Nothing like the ones on the drawing. The human-lion guardian must mean something else."

Carlton looked crestfallen.

"Hey, don't sweat it," I told him. "You found a

reference to the pillars and the cryptic line about opening a gate. That's going to be useful. The pillars aren't under the Sphinx but we'll find out where they are. Good job."

A flicker of a smile crossed his lips. "Thanks." He looked at my shoulder as if noticing it for the first time. "What happened to you?"

"I got scratched by a ghoul."

Understanding flashed in his eyes. "So that's why you were asking about ghouls on the phone?"

I nodded.

"But there's no cure for ghoul poison. Oh my god are you going to..?" His words trailed off, leaving the question unasked.

"I'm fine," I said. "It turns out there is a cure for ghoul poison after all."

He examined the poultice briefly before pulling his head away from it. "Is that where the bad smell is coming from?"

"Yeah, you don't want to get too close."

"I guess I should get home anyway," he said. "My wife will be waiting for me. I'll see you guys tomorrow." He gave Leon a wave and walked to the front door with a sad look on his face.

"Hey, Carlton, don't feel bad," I said, following him to the door. "You gave us some great information. We can work with that."

He shrugged and said, "I guess you guys will be working tonight, huh?"

"Yeah, that's the plan."

"Cool," he said flatly. "I guess I'll go home then." He stepped out into the rain and walked toward his house with his head down and shoulders hunched.

Did he feel bad because I hadn't asked him to join us? Maybe he was feeling left out.

"Hey," I called after him. "We're gonna order pizza, have a few beers, and go through the books. Do you want to join us?"

He turned to face me, a grin on his face. "Yeah, I'd like that. Can I bring my wife?"

"Err…yeah, I guess."

"Great! I'll go and get her." He sprinted through the rain to his house. When he got to the door, he turned to face me again. "Muriel likes pineapple on her pizza."

Before I could reply, he disappeared into the house.

I went back to the living room where Leon was leafing through one of the texts. "Carlton and his wife are going to be joining us."

He pointed at my bare chest, grinning. "Maybe you should put a shirt on. You want to make a good first impression, don't you?"

He had a point. I went up to the bedroom and got a blue flannel shirt out of the closet. Before I put it on, I washed the poultice off my shoulder at the bathroom sink and applied a little cologne to my shoulder to make sure no remnant of the foul smell remained.

When I got back downstairs, Carlton was standing in the living room with a tall mousy-haired woman dressed in dark slacks and a white sweater.

"Alec," Carlton said cheerily. "This is my wife Muriel. Muriel, this is Alec Harbinger."

"Pleased to meet you," she said with a smile. "Carlton has told me so much about you. He's thrilled to be a part of your team."

"Nice to meet you too," I said.

"I also told her that if she smells anything bad, it's just the poultice on your shoulder," Carlton said with a wink.

"You have such an exciting job," Muriel said. "And so dangerous. I can't even imagine how many times you must have escaped death. Unfortunately, some of the people Carlton has worked with in the past haven't been so lucky."

"So we heard," Leon said, looking up from his book.

"Well it's a dangerous business," Muriel said, going over to Leon with her hand outstretched. "And you are?"

"Leon Smith," he said, getting up and shaking her hand. "I'm Alec's friend."

"Well, I'm willing to help out any way I can," she said. "Carlton said you're doing some research into some pillars." She pointed at the drawing on the wall. "I assume it's these you're looking for?"

"That's right," I said. "We need to comb through the books and see if we can find any reference to the pillars. This is one of the less exciting aspects of the job."

"Nonsense," she said. "Work like this is the backbone of what you do. You venture into monsters' lairs and kill them but it's the research that gets you there in the first place, eh?"

"I guess so," I said. I gestured to the books. "If you guys want to start reading, I'll order the pizzas."

"Could we get one with pineapple?" Muriel asked. "I just love pineapple on a pizza."

"Coming right up," I said, speed-dialing the pizza place.

After I placed the order, I went to the fridge and got four beers. Leon, Carlton, and Muriel had their heads buried in the books and the living room was as quiet as a library. Only the rain tapping on the window broke the silence.

I found a book I hadn't looked at yet—*A Magical History of Giza*—and sat on the floor while I scanned through its pages. Half an hour and a beer later, I still hadn't found anything useful and, judging by the silence in the room, neither had anyone else.

A light rap sounded at the door. "Pizza guy," I said, getting up and stretching.

I went to the door and paid for the two pizzas —a Pepperoni and a Hawaiian—before bringing them back to the living room and placing them side by side on the table.

"I take it no one has found anything useful yet," I said.

No one had.

"I still think the human-lion guardian refers to the Sphinx," Carlton said. "It has to. Nothing else makes sense."

"There's nothing like those pillars under the Sphinx," I said. "There are tunnels running all over the Giza Plateau and maybe the pillars are in one that hasn't been discovered yet but they definitely aren't beneath the Sphinx."

Muriel reached for one of the pizza boxes and opened it. When she saw the Pepperoni pie inside instead of the Hawaiian, she closed the box again and pushed it away. "Wrong one," she said.

I looked at the two identical pizza boxes on the table and a memory came to me; something I'd read during an Egyptology lesson when I was training to become a P.I.

"Carlton, I think you're right," I said, my eyes

fixed on the two boxes. "The Pillars of Khonsu are in a subterranean room beneath the Sphinx."

He looked confused. "But you just said—"

"I know what I said and I was right. No exploration beneath the Sphinx has revealed pillars like the ones we're looking for. They're not there."

Leon raised a quizzical eyebrow. "Okay, now I'm confused."

"The human-lion guardian has to mean the Sphinx." I said. "Anything else wouldn't make sense." I pulled up an image of the Sphinx on my phone and held it up so everyone could see it. "A lion's body and a human head," I said. "There's nothing else like it."

"So the pillars are under there," Carlton said. "I knew it."

"No, they're not."

He sat back and let out a sigh. "What am I missing?"

"There's nothing else like the Sphinx in modern times," I said. "It's unique. But there's a widely held belief that there were once two Sphinxes. One of them either collapsed or the stones were repurposed and used to build other structures on the Plateau. Carlton is right; the Pillars of Khonsu are beneath the Sphinx." I gestured at the picture on my phone. "But they're not underneath *this* Sphinx; they're under the one that's no longer there."

"Where the hell is that?" Leon asked.

"There's an area where excavations have revealed a foundation beneath the sand. Some people believe it's the foundation of a second Sphinx."

"So the room with the pillars is under there," Carlton said. "That makes sense."

I went over to the crude drawing on the wall. "The pillars are obviously a gate of some kind. Since Tia thinks we need to find the pillars to get to her mummy, I assume they're a gateway to the realm in which Rekhmire resides."

"Great," Carlton said. "I'll book a flight to Egypt for you."

"It isn't that simple. From the description Carlton found, it seems that some sort of words are needed to open the gate. We don't know what those words are."

"A prayer that cannot be spoken in the day or night," Leon said.

"Exactly."

"So what do we do now?" Muriel asked.

"We hit the books again," I said. "We know where the pillars are. Now we need to find out how to open the gate."

It was going to take more than one night to crack the riddle of the pillars. It was almost midnight when I put my book down and I still hadn't found anything that could help us get to Tia's mummy.

We'd eaten the pizzas, drunk a couple of beers each, and pored over the texts but the prayer that could not be spoken in the day or night refused to be found.

"I'm beat," Leon said, closing the text he'd been reading. "I'm going to go home and pick this up tomorrow."

"I guess we should head home too, eh?" Carlton said to Muriel.

She nodded and put her book aside. With a sigh of resignation, she said, "Yes, we should. I have to get up early tomorrow. I have to meet my new students."

"You're a teacher?" I asked.

"A music teacher," she said. "And I start my new job tomorrow so we really should be going."

"Sure," I said, getting up from the floor and stretching my aching joints. "Thanks for your help."

"It's just a shame we didn't find anything useful," she said as she and Carlton walked to the front door. The rain had finally stopped but the night air was cold and it rushed into the house when Muriel opened the door.

"Goodnight," Carlton said as they stepped outside. "I'll see you tomorrow."

"Yeah," I said. "See you tomorrow." My attention was drawn to a dark green Ford Taurus parked across the road. I could see two men inside—one with dark hair, the other blond—and they seemed to be trying to sit stock still so as not to attract any attention to themselves.

Too late.

I didn't let them know I'd spotted them by lingering at the door for too long. I closed it and went back to the living room.

Leon was on his feet, stretching and yawning. "I'm going to get some sleep," he said. "The writing style in those books is very dry. I'll be dreaming about Egyptian architecture tonight."

"We may have a problem," I said.

The tiredness was gone from his face instantly. "What is it?"

"Two guys parked across the street in a green Taurus."

He surreptitiously glanced out of the window. "I see them. What are they doing there?"

"Watching the house."

"Why?"

I shrugged. "No idea. But the wards I set up on the street haven't been tripped, which means one of two things. Either they don't mean any harm or they're skilled enough to get past my wards without setting them off. If it's the latter, they're pretty good."

"So what are you gonna do? Go over there and see who they are?"

"I don't feel comfortable confronting them on the street. If they're good enough to slip past my wards, they probably have a lot of power. If a confrontation escalated into a fight, there could be collateral damage. I won't let that happen. Maybe I'll take a drive out of town, see if they follow."

"Want some company?"

"I thought you were tired."

"Who needs sleep when there are bad guys' asses to kick?"

I grinned. "Sure, let's go for a ride."

We left the house and got into the Land Rover. As I backed onto the street, I made sure to keep my attention away from the Taurus. No need to let them know I was onto them, even though they were pretty conspicuous. They might have enough knowledge to get past the wards but they needed a lesson in looking inconspicuous.

"Where are we going?' Leon asked as we got to the end of the street. I checked the rearview mirror. The Taurus hadn't moved.

"Far enough away that we can deal with them without having to worry about property damage." My presence in Dearmont had brought enough danger to the town when John DuMont, a traitor within the Society, had tried to raise a zombie army here. If these guys were intent on causing trouble, I'd make sure they caused it far away from innocent people.

I turned onto the next street and checked behind me again. No headlights. Maybe I'd been wrong about them after all and their presence on the street was totally innocent.

Then I saw them turn out of my street and follow us, keeping their distance.

"They don't know we're onto them," I said to Leon. "They're keeping back, trying to be inconspicuous."

"It's a little late for that," he said. "So what's

the plan? We lead them out of town and then run them off the road? Beat them up some before we tell them to stay the hell away?"

"I thought we might find out who they are first. We'll get out of town and pull over somewhere where it's quiet. They'll probably drive right past us so they don't blow their cover. We'll stop their car and question them."

He raised an eyebrow. "How are we gonna stop their car? You have some magical device that will turn off their engine or something?"

"No, but I have a big sword in the trunk. If I stand on the road in front of them, they're either going to try and run me down or try to get away. Either way, I'll slice their engine block and stop them I've done it before and it works every time."

He laughed. "Yeah, I bet it does. Cool. So we question them and find out who they are and what they want."

I nodded. "We just have to find a quiet stretch of road."

"Shouldn't be too hard at this time of night."

"That's what I'm hoping."

We drove through town with the Taurus in pursuit. It hung back at every stoplight but didn't let us get too far enough away that we were out of sight. The driver was good at this and in any other circumstances—if it wasn't the dead of night with barely any traffic on the road and if I hadn't already been aware of him—he'd be all but invisible.

When I hit the highway, I headed north. The Taurus, of course, followed.

The driver's skill in tailing us would also be his downfall. The fact that he was so far behind the Land Rover meant that I'd have plenty of time to pull over and get the sword out of the back before the Taurus reached us. Once I had the sword in my hand, our pursuers weren't going anywhere.

Ten minutes later, I pulled over and got out. Leon joined me at the tailgate and we each took a sword from the variety of weapons in the trunk.

"When the car gets here, I'll stand in front of it," I said. "You get on the road behind it in case they try to back up."

"Okay," Leon said, moving into the trees by the side of the road so he wouldn't be seen before heading back the way we'd come.

I waited by the Land Rover, sword in hand.

The headlights of the Taurus cut through the night and illuminated me. I imagined the confusion on the driver's face, even though I couldn't see anything past the glare of the lights. This was the moment of truth. The men in the Taurus knew I'd seen them. They would probably try to run.

I tightened my grip on the sword, waiting for the Taurus to speed up.

It didn't. Instead, it slowed down and came to a stop behind the Land Rover. The driver turned off the lights and both men got out.

"There's no need for any trouble, Harbinger," one of them said.

"Why are you following me?"

Leon was walking back along the road. If this turned nasty, at least I'd have backup.

The two men were getting closer. "Stop right there," I said. "Tell me who the hell you are and why you were outside my house."

They stopped in their tracks but didn't say anything.

I raised the tip of the sword slightly. "I'm waiting."

"We just want to talk," the dark-haired one said.

"You have a strange way of introducing yourself. If you want to talk, why not knock on my door instead of lurking outside my house?"

"We were working up to it," the blond guy said. "We weren't staking out your house or anything. We'd only just arrived when you opened your front door and obviously saw us. We were going to knock."

"But instead, you tailed me all the way out here."

"Okay, I'll be honest with you," the dark-haired guy said. "We were hesitating because we want to do a deal with you but we know that because of who we are, you might not want to do that."

I frowned, confused. "What do you mean? Who are you?"

"I'm Tom Meyer," the blond one said. "And this is Doug Chance. We're members of the Midnight Cabal."

13

Felicity parked the Ford Focus in front of Jessica Baker's house. Her shoulders, back, and legs were sore and she could still feel the sting of the tattoo gun. The outlines of the protective symbols had been tattooed onto her body and she had another appointment in a couple of weeks to get them filled in.

According to Deb, the outlines were the worst part and the filling in was much easier to endure. Felicity hadn't found today's procedure grueling or anything like that but it had been uncomfortable. With the magical symbols inked on her skin, she felt like a real P.I. Deb had said that even though the symbols were only outlines at the moment, they worked just as effectively as they would when they were filled in.

As she was about to get out of the car, Felicity's phone rang. She fished it out of her handbag and checked the number. Unknown. She answered it, hoping it wasn't some sort of telemarketing call. She was surprised to hear the voice of Nigel Lomas, the man who'd given her the keys to her office, house, and car at Mysterium Imports in London before she'd travelled to Manchester.

"How are things?" he asked.

"Great. I've got a case already."

"Oh."

Oh? That wasn't the reaction she'd expected.

"Is something wrong?" she asked.

There was a pause and then Lomas said, "What kind of case?"

"I don't know yet; I haven't spoken to the client about the details yet."

"I want you to contact a P.I. named Mike Fawkes and give him the details once you've got them." He gave her Mike's phone number and the address of his office, which was a few miles away from her own.

What the hell was going on? This was her first case; why would she give it to someone else? "I don't understand," she told Lomas.

"You're brand new to all of this," he said. "A freshly minted P.I. You're going to need some help. There must be plenty to do around the office. I thought you'd be sticking around the there for a while, getting it fit for purpose."

"But I have a case." What was he talking about? She became a P.I. to help people, not to clean up the office. She'd planned to hire a local cleaning company to get the office into shape and then she was going to bill the Society for it. But Nigel Lomas thought she should do that herself and pass her case on to another P.I.? Her grip tightened around the phone.

"You can interview the client," he said. "Bring her into the office and explain that the office is being refurbished. Then pass the details of the case onto Mike."

How did Lomas know her client was a woman? Was her phone being tapped? Was she being watched?

She turned in her seat and checked for the black van. There it was, parked among a row of other cars behind her.

"Do you know anything about a black van that's following me?" she said into the phone.

"No," Lomas said, without missing a beat. "I don't."

He hadn't asked her what van she was talking about or why she thought she was being followed. He'd merely denied any knowledge of the vehicle immediately.

What was going on?

As she watched, the black van pulled away from the curb, drove past her car, and turned left at the end of the street, disappearing from view. Had the driver just received a phone call from the Society telling him he'd been spotted? Or was she just being paranoid? Why would the Society be spying on her? It didn't make sense.

"I have to go now," she said.

"Don't forget, you need to pass on the--"

Felicity ended the call.

She sat in the bubble of silence within the car for a moment, her mind replaying the conversation she'd just had with Nigel Lomas. Why would the Society bring her over to England and carry out surveillance on her? Why did Lomas want her to stay at the office?

A thought crossed her mind that made her feel sick. Had she been promoted to P.I. because the Society thought she was good enough or because it suited their purposes?

There was obviously more going on than she'd been led to believe.

She got out of the car and pushed through a small wooden gate that opened into Jessica Baker's front garden. A concrete path cut through the small lawn to the front door.

Before Felicity reached the door, it opened and a woman who looked to be in her late thirties smiled at her. "You must be Felicity. I'm Jessica. Thanks for coming."

She was dressed in jeans and a baggy gray sweater. Her black hair was scraped back into a pony tail. She looked tired, as if she hadn't slept for a while.

She led Felicity into a small living room and indicated a dark green sofa that had seen better days. "Sit down and I'll make us a tea."

Felicity sat, took her notebook out of her handbag, and let her eyes wander the room. A number of framed photos sat on a wooden mantelpiece over the gas fire. Most of them showed Jessica with a slim dark-haired man Felicity assumed was her husband. The pictures had been taken while the couple were on holiday. Spain, Felicity guessed, judging from the scenery.

Her guess was confirmed when she saw the Sagrada Familia church in the background of one of the pictures.

Jessica returned with two mugs of tea and placed one on the coffee table in front of Felicity. She looked at the pictures and smiled. "Those were taken last year when we went on holiday to Barcelona. That's my husband Rob."

"Looks like you had a nice time," Felicity said. She took a quick sip of the scalding tea and turned to face Jessica, who'd taken a seat next to her on the sofa. "You said on the phone that you have a problem."

"That's right," Jessica said. "I'll just come right out and say it. I'm being haunted." She grimaced. "You probably think I'm crazy now, don't you?"

"No, not at all," Felicity said. She did, however, feel a sinking feeling in her stomach. If Jessica's case had involved a flesh and blood preternatural creature, there would be physical evidence that could be examined, traits that could be researched to find the creature. With a ghost, there wouldn't be any physical evidence at all and it would be difficult to prove that Jessica was actually being haunted and didn't just have an overactive imagination.

"Tell me more," she said. "When did this haunting start?"

"A couple of weeks ago, when my mother died. Her name was Linda Dean. It's her that's haunting me, you see. The first time I saw her was at the cemetery where she's buried. She was standing in the trees, gesturing to me. Rob was with me at the time but he didn't see anything. So at first I thought it was just stress or something that was making me imagine her. Part of the bereavement process. But then I started to see her in the house at night."

"Did Rob see her as well this time?" Felicity

asked. Without some sort of corroboration, it was going to be difficult to accept Jessica's story.

"No, he wasn't here. He works for a delivery firm and he's out at all hours." She looked closely at Felicity. "You don't believe me, do you? You think that because I'm the only person who saw her, I must be imagining it."

"I don't think that at all," Felicity assured her. "It just would have been nice if someone else has seen the ghost as well."

"Someone else did," Jessica said. "Charlie, the groundskeeper at the cemetery. He saw her one night. He wasn't going to tell me because he thought it would upset me but when I told him I'd seen her ghost in the house, he said he'd seen her as well. She'd been standing by the trees in the cemetery one night."

Felicity made a note. "Do you know Charlie's full name?"

Jessica shrugged. "No, he's just Charlie. He's been working at the cemetery for years. I first started talking to him after my dad died. That was ten years ago."

"And the name of the cemetery?"

"It's the one on Cedar Street, not far from here. I can take you there if you like and we can talk to Charlie. He'll confirm what I just told you."

Speaking to an independent witness would

definitely be helpful but Felicity wanted more details first. "Perhaps after I get some more information. How did your mother die, if you don't mind me asking."

Jessica's lips began to quiver and her eyes filled with tears. "She was murdered. Her body was found in the canal. At first the police thought she'd fallen in and drowned. It happens a lot. But the postmortem revealed that she'd been strangled and then pushed in. They've got no clue where she was actually killed because she'd...drifted for a couple of days before she was found."

"I'm sorry," Felicity said, placing a comforting hand gently on Jessica's arm. "That sounds terrible."

Jessica nodded and wiped her eyes. "It is. I sometimes wonder if that's why she's a ghost now, because she suffered a violent death. A psychic medium told me that's how ghosts are created. They wander around, trapped here until the injustice that was done to them is righted."

"Where exactly do you see her in the house?" Felicity asked.

"In my bedroom usually. She's standing over my bed and trying to tell me something but there's no sound coming out of her mouth."

"And how do you react? Are you scared?"

"No, I'm not scared. She's my mother. She'd

never harm me. She sometimes stands at the foot of the bed and points out of the window, as if she's trying to show me something."

"What is she trying to show you?"

"I don't know. The first time she did it, I turned the light on and she vanished. I can only see her in the dark. The next time, I went to the window and looked out. But there's nothing out there except the other houses on the street."

"Do you mind if I have a look?"

"Of course. It's this way but you'll have to excuse the mess." Jessica got up and took Felicity upstairs to the bedroom.

The room was small but cozy with a double bed and a dressing table. Because the bedroom was at the front of the house, the window looked out onto the street. Felicity had no idea what the ghost of Linda Dean was trying to show her daughter. She looked beyond the street. There were more houses and then fields in the distance."

"See," Jessica said. "There's nothing out there."

"What does the ghost do after she points out of the window."

"Nothing. I tell her I don't know what she's trying to tell me and she seems to get frustrated and disappears."

Felicity took a photo of the view from the window on her phone just in case there was something she was missing. It was better to be thorough than overlook a vital clue.

"Perhaps we should talk to Charlie at the cemetery," she said.

"Yeah, that'd be a good idea," Jessica said. "At least you'll know I'm not making all this up."

"I already believe you." And that was true; she did believe what she was being told. The ghost's actions were too specific for this to be a figment of Jessica's imagination. Felicity had heard that ghosts sometimes had unfinished business and that certainly seemed to be the case here. Like the psychic medium had told Jessica, her mother might be trapped here until the wrong that had been done to her was righted.

They went back downstairs and Jessica said, "We can walk to the cemetery if you like. It isn't far. Only up the road."

"Yes, that'd be nice." She wanted to find out what Jessica knew about the P.I. who worked out of the office before her and a walk would give her plenty of opportunity to broach the subject.

Outside, there was a chill in the air but no sign of rain. That had thankfully stopped by the time Felicity had left the tattoo studio. They walked along the street in silence for a moment and then Felicity said, "When you called my office a week ago, do you remember who was working there at the time?"

"He never called me back so I didn't speak to him."

"But do you remember his name?"

"No, sorry. Oh, hang on." She dug inside her handbag and brought out a phone. "When I saved the number on my phone, I put the name of the business in my Contacts. It's always your name isn't it? Like if I was a P.I. it would be Baker P.I."

"That's right," Felicity said, remembering her excitement at seeing the words *Lake P.I.* on the frosted glass of the door.

"Just give me a minute and I'll find it," Jessica said, scrolling through her Contacts list. "Here it is. Fawkes P.I. That's it, I remember now. His name was Mike Fawkes."

14

"Maybe we could go somewhere else to talk," Meyer said. "I don't feel comfortable conducting business at the side of the road."

I scoffed. "What business do you think we're conducting?" If he thought I was going to deal with the Midnight Cabal, he was mistaken.

"Like I said, can we go somewhere else to discuss this?"

"No," I said. "And stop following me." I turned to the Land Rover and waited for Leon to join me.

As I opened the door, Meyer said, "You can't get through the pillars of Khonsu without us."

That made me pause. I turned to face him. "What are you talking about?"

"You know exactly what I'm talking about. You're trying to get through the Pillars of Khonsu to save your friend. We know you're looking for them. But only we know how to open the gate."

I looked at Leon. He gave me an almost imperceptible shrug. We were both thinking the same thing; how did the Midnight Cabal know what we were doing? I was sure that the same name came into both of our heads at the same time. Carlton Carmichael.

I trusted everyone who had been at the meeting at my house except for Carlton and Merlin. There was no way Merlin would speak to the Cabal because he hated them but I couldn't be so sure about Carlton. Was he a mole who had been planted into my team to report back to the sworn enemies of the Society?

"Come on," Meyer said, sensing my hesitation. "Let's talk."

I supposed there was no harm in hearing what they had to say. "Okay," I said.

Chance, the dark-haired guy, said, "There's a diner a little farther along the road. We can talk there."

"Sure," I said, getting into the Land Rover after stowing my sword on the back seat.

Leon did the same and slid into the passenger seat. "We're not really going to deal with those guys are we?"

"We'll see what they have to say."

"Whatever it is, it won't be good."

"Probably not but if I walk away without checking out what they have to say and they have some important information that might save Mallory, I'd never forgive myself. I made the mistake of not checking out all possibilities a couple of nights ago and those two police officers ended up in the hospital because of it."

"Okay, I get you. But I don't think anything good is going to come from talking to the Midnight Cabal. Also, were you thinking what I was thinking when they knew so much about what we've been doing?"

"Yeah," I said.

"So Carlton must be a spy. Or maybe his wife is. Hell, they probably both are."

"I'll deal with him tomorrow," I said. "Right now, let's see if these two know something that will save Mallory."

The Taurus drove past us. I followed it to Darla's Diner. When we got to the parking lot, Meyer and Chance nodded curtly to us but didn't speak. We all went inside.

At this time of night, Darla's wasn't busy. There were a few truck drivers in the place but that was all. Meyer and Chance slid into a booth by the window. Leon and I joined them, facing them across the table.

The waitress came over and took our order

for four coffees. After she'd filled our cups from the pot, she left us to it.

"So talk," I said, looking from Meyer to Chance.

"We know you want to get through the Pillars of Khonsu," Meyer said.

"To save your friend from some kind of curse," Chance added.

"The only way to open the gate is a specific spell." Meyer said. "There is no way on earth you can find that spell. It's in the possession of our organization and for the last few hundred years, the Midnight Cabal has made sure that the spell has been removed from all other texts that might have mentioned it. The only copy of it is in our hands."

"I've already found a mention of the spell," I said.

Chance laughed. "Of course you have. The prayer that cannot be spoken in the day or night, right? Yeah, it's mentioned in plenty of places but the actual spell is nowhere to be found."

"Except we have it," Meyer added.

"Great," I said. "Give it to me and you'll save me a lot of pointless searching."

Meyer chuckled. "It isn't that simple, Harbinger. We're not going to just give you the spell."

"Wow, that's a surprise," Leon said.

"But we were thinking," Chance said. "Maybe we help you and you help us."

He waited for a reaction. Neither Leon nor I gave him one.

"We want to go through the Pillars too," Meyer said. "In fact, that's why our organization has jealously guarded the key that opens the gate. We want what's on the other side."

I quirked an eyebrow at him. "And what is that?"

"We're not exactly sure. We're hoping to find artifacts there."

"So you want to loot the place?"

Chance took a sip of his coffee and then said, "That's a crude way of putting it but yes, we want to loot the place."

"Aren't you forgetting something important? I'm not sure Rekhmire is going to let you walk off with all his stuff."

Chance looked at Meyer and said, "He doesn't know."

Meyer shook his head. "No, I don't think he does."

I wasn't going to give them the satisfaction of knowing I was curious. So I slowly drank some coffee before causally saying, "I don't know what?"

"Rekhmire isn't a threat," Meyer said. "He's locked away in a magical prison. It seems that rising up against Pharaoh Amanhotep wasn't a smart move. After defeating the army of the dead, the Pharaoh had Rekhmire sealed away behind a magical barrier."

Chance cut in. "So not only is Rekhmire in a realm which can only be reached by going through the Pillars of Khonsu, he's in a prison within that realm. He's no threat at all."

"It seems to me he was a threat when he was somehow working with John DuMont to raise an army of the dead here in Dearmont."

"DuMont made contact with Rekhmire by magical means. More of a psychic connection than anything else. And that was only achievable because DuMont had the Staff of Midnight. Trust me, Rekhmire is locked away."

"But that's the problem," I said. "I don't trust you."

Chance shrugged. "Of course you don't. We come from two organizations that are diametrically opposed. Why should we trust each other? We shouldn't. But if we have the same goal, why couldn't we put our differences aside?"

"If you know how to get through the gate and Rekhmire's no problem," Leon said, "Then why do you need our help? Why haven't you gone through already and ripped Rekhmire off?"

It was a good question but I was sure I already

knew the answer. "Because they don't know where the Pillars are," I said.

Meyer nodded. "That's true. However, we have reason to believe you may know. You know where the Pillars are, we know how to get through the gate. We each hold half of the key. So why not work together to achieve our separate goals?"

I looked at Leon and he looked at me and I was sure we were both thinking the same thing again. Carlton knew the Pillars were under the foundation of the second Sphinx, the one that no longer existed. If he was reporting to the Cabal, then why didn't they know the location already? Why were they trying to make a deal?

Maybe I was wrong about Carlton.

Regardless, if working with the Midnight Cabal was the only chance I had of getting through the gate and saving Mallory's life, I had to take it. I couldn't let her die just because I was too proud to form an uneasy alliance with my enemies.

I had no doubt that the Cabal would try to screw us over in some way. I couldn't even take their word for it that Rekhmire was in some kind of prison on the other side of the gate. But those were problems I'd have to deal with as they arose. Right now, the important thing was getting through the gate so Mallory could put the heart back into Tia's mummy and break the death curse.

"Tell me exactly what you're proposing," I said to the two Cabal members.

"It's simple," Meyer said. "We all go to the Pillars together. Doug and I will cast the spell to open the gate. We all go through together. While we're on the other side, we look for artifacts while you save your friend. Then we all come back through the gate and go our separate ways."

"Nothing could be simpler," Chance added.

"What's to stop you attacking us once we take you to the gate?"

"A big strong guy like you?" Meyer asked. "What's to stop you attacking us once we open the gate?"

"There has to be an element of trust or this won't work." Chance said.

"First I have to trust that there are no other copies of the spell out there," I said. "You might just be telling me that so I get you to the Pillars."

Meyer sighed. "Believe me, the Midnight Cabal has done all it can over the last few centuries to erase that spell from all the texts in existence. You won't find it."

He might be lying or he might be telling the truth. I could tell him to shove it and continue the search for the prayer that opened the gate. Maybe I'd find it and maybe I wouldn't. But with

Mallory's life on the line, I couldn't take that chance.

The two officers from the cemetery were in hospital because I'd taken a chance and not checked for more ghouls in the tunnels. I'd regret that they got hurt because of my actions for the rest of my life.

I wasn't about to make the same mistake with Mallory. Her life was on the line.

"Okay," I said to Meyer and Chance. "I'll do it."

"Excellent," Meyer said. "We're ready when you are."

"Tomorrow," I said. "Be at my house at--"

"Wait," Chance said, holding up a hand to stop me. He took his phone out of his pocket and went to the Calculator app. He made a couple of calculations. "It can't be tomorrow."

"Why?" I asked.

"The spell that opens the gate has to be cast at twilight."

"Neither the day nor the night," Meyer explained.

"And we'll never make it to Egypt in time," Chance said. "The Pillars are in Egypt, right?"

"They are," I said. "So what time will it be here when it's twilight in Egypt?"

He did another quick calculation. "12:20 in the afternoon."

"Be at my house by 11:30."

He frowned at me. "What? I don't understand."

"Just be there."

They looked at each other and shrugged.

"Don't be late," I told them as I got up.

Leon and I left the diner and went back to the Land Rover. When we got in the car, he said, "Do you think that was a good idea? You know they're going to double cross us."

"I know but I didn't see any other option." I started the engine and drove out of the parking lot.

As we drove along the highway toward Dearmont, Leon said, "Well now you know how Faust felt."

"Faust?"

"Yeah, Faust. He also made a deal with the devil."

15

The cemetery near Jessica Baker's house was neat, tidy, and surrounded by trees. Felicity followed Jessica along a gravel path that wound between the rows of headstones.

She was still wondering why Nigel Lomas had told her to pass her case to Mike Fawkes, the P.I. who had worked in the office before her. If she was supposed to hand him her case, then why wasn't he still in the office? Why had he moved out?

"It's down here," Jessica said, stepping off the path and walking toward the trees. She stopped at a simple gray headstone that bore the name Linda Dean and the dates of her birth and death.

"Dad is right next to her," Jessica said, indicating a stone that bore the name Frank Dean and his notable dates. As Jessica had said, he'd died ten years ago.

"You said you saw the ghost when you were standing here?" Felicity asked.

Jessica nodded. "It was the night after she was buried. Rob was away on a job and I had nothing to do so I came here and sat on the grass by the grave. That was when I saw her in the trees over there."

Felicity followed Jessica's pointing finger. Trees had been planted around the edge of the graveyard. They kept out the noise of the traffic on the roads and made the place seem more tranquil.

"She was gesturing to me," Jessica said. "I was scared and I ran home. I feel silly now. After that, she started visiting me at home."

Felicity looked down at the grave. If Jessica wanted to stop the haunting, then Felicity would have to come back here at nighttime when there was no one else around and salt the bones. But she wasn't sure Jessica wanted to stop the haunting.

"You want to know what she's trying to tell you, don't you?" she said.

Jessica turned to face her and there were tears in her eyes again. "Yes. I think it's something important. She keeps trying to tell me but I don't know what she's trying to say."

Felicity wasn't confident that she could help. She was hardly the ghost whisperer.

"Can you help me?" Jessica asked.

Felicity looked at the woman in front of her; at the tiredness in her eyes and the sense of anguish that seemed to surround her regarding the subject of her mother.

"I'll try. I can't promise anything but I'll try to help you."

"Oh, thank you." Jessica drew her into a quick hug. "I can't bear the thought that she's trying to say something important--something important enough to bring her back from the grave--and I can't understand her."

"Don't worry. We'll get to the bottom of it." One thing was for sure; she wasn't passing Jessica's case on to Mike Fawkes. "Now, would it be possible to speak to the groundskeeper?"

"Yes, I'm sure he's here somewhere," Jessica said, looking around. "He usually is."

"Is that him over there?" Felicity pointed at a man tending the flowers on a grave near the path.

"Yes, that's him." Jessica led Felicity to him.

When the man saw them approaching, he stood up and touched the brim of his tweed cap. "Afternoon, ladies." He was dressed for the weather in a dark green wax jacket, black trousers, and black boots. A wheelbarrow by his side contained an array of gardening tools.

"Hello, Charlie," Jessica said. "This is Felicity. She wants to talk to you about the time you saw Mum's ghost."

"Oh, right. I could tell you were a believer as soon as I saw you."

"I've seen a lot of things," Felicity said. "I'm quite open-minded."

"Yes I'm sure you are. Now then, the time I saw Mrs Dean, it was about half past eleven at night. I was walking along this path here and I saw a figure standing in the trees over there. The cemetery was closed and that means the big iron gate was shut so I knew it wasn't someone coming to pay their respects to a loved one."

He took off his hat and scratched his balding head. "I went over there thinking someone had sneaked in and I was going to have to chuck them out. But as I got closer, I realized it was Mrs Dean. I knew who she was, of course; she often came to visit her husband's grave. Anyway, as I got closer, she disappeared into the trees there."

"She didn't try to talk to you?" Felicity asked. "Or did she point at anything?"

He shook his head. "No, like I said, she just vanished. There's not really anything else I can tell you, I'm afraid. One minute she was there and the next, she was gone."

"Thank you," Felicity said. "Can I just get your

full name for my notes?" She took her notebook out of her pocket.

He smiled. "Of course. It's Charlie Sutherland."

Felicity wrote down the name. "Thanks, you've been a great help."

"Thanks, Charlie," Jessica said. She and Felicity walked along the path toward the entrance. Felicity saw the big iron gates Charlie had mentioned and was glad she didn't need to come back and salt the bones after all. She didn't fancy climbing those. Or the high wall that marked the cemetery's perimeter beyond the trees.

Out of the blue, Jessica asked, "Do you think my mum knows who killed her?"

Felicity wasn't sure where that question had come from. "I don't know. Why do you ask?"

"Maybe that's what she's trying to tell me."

"Do the police have any leads?"

"No. They said the problem is that they don't even know where she was killed. So they haven't got a crime scene to investigate. We're just hoping someone finds her necklace. Then the police will know where to look."

"Her necklace?"

Jessica nodded solemnly. "She always wore a silver necklace that was shaped like a heart. Dad got it for her on her 40th birthday. It has her initials engraved on it. She wasn't wearing it when she was found. If it didn't come off in the canal, then it could be at the crime scene. Or the person who strangled her might have taken it home as a trophy or something."

"I see," Felicity said.

"So I wonder if she's trying to tell me where it is."

"We'll try and find out." They'd reached Jessica's house. Felicity said, "I think the best thing is for me to try and see your mother's ghost for myself. Does she come to the house every night?"

"No," Jessica said. "You're welcome to come over but it will have to be a time when Rob is at work. He doesn't like me talking about the haunting at all. He thinks I'm going crazy and he says that scares him. So I don't talk about it at all with him."

"Oh. Maybe I should go to the cemetery tonight then. There's a chance I might see her there, I suppose. Do you think Charlie would let me in?"

Jessica thought about that for a second and then said, "I'm sure he will. He's really nice. After my dad died, Charlie talked to me every time I went to the grave and he really helped. I'm sure he'll let you into the cemetery if you ask him."

"All right, I will. I'll be in touch tomorrow and

let you know how I got on."

Jessica nodded. "Okay. Thank you for all your help."

Felicity smiled and watched as Jessica went back into the house. She didn't feel like she deserved any thanks yet. She hadn't done anything to help Jessica and from what she knew about the case, it was going to be a hard one. Ghosts were definitely not her specialty.

She got into the Focus and drove back to the cemetery. She walked through the open gates and went in search of Charlie Sutherland. He wasn't where she'd last seen him. Now, he and his wheelbarrow were farther along the path, toward the rear of the cemetery.

He saw Felicity approaching and touched the brim of his cap, as he'd done before. "Hello again."

"Hello." she said. "I was wondering if it would be possible for me to come here tonight and wait around to see if Linda Dean's ghost appears."

He stroked his chin and looked toward the gates, seemingly considering. "Well, I suppose I don't see why not. You're doing this to help Jessica aren't you?"

She nodded. "Yes, I am."

"All right. That poor young lady has had a bad time lately with her mother being killed like that. If you're trying to help her, then I'm willing to help you. I'll close the gates but I'll leave them unlocked. Just push them open when you get here. But close them after yourself. I can't have just anyone coming in here at night."

"I'll do that," Felicity told him.

"All right then. I hope you find something useful."

"Thank you." She went back to the car and got in. Before driving back to the office, she found Mike Fawkes' phone number, which she'd jotted down when Nigel Lomas had given it to her, and rang it.

A voice that sounded younger than Felicity had expected answered. "Mike Fawkes, P.I."

"Hello, Mike. My name is Felicity Lake and I was given your number by--"

"Nigel Lomas," he said. "I was told to expect your call. I understand you have a case for me."

"No, actually, I haven't. That turned out to be a dead end."

"Oh, okay. Is that why you're calling? To tell me that?"

"No, I'm calling because I seem to have taken over your old office and I'm wondering why I'm supposed to pass my cases onto you."

He sighed. "Hell if I know. A couple of days ago, Nigel told me they needed my office so they kicked me out. Now I'm in a place half the size and my filing cabinets are taking up most of what little space there is."

Knowing how small the office Fawkes had moved from was, Felicity could imagine the place he was in now.

"So why have they done it?" she asked.

"Like I said, I have no idea. I'm only enduring it because Nigel said it wouldn't be for long and then I'd be going back to my old office."

"Oh," Felicity said. What did that mean for her? Was she going to be sent somewhere else soon? No one had mentioned that when she'd arrived in England.

"Sorry I can't be of more help," Fawkes said. "If you get any cases, throw them my way. For some reason, Nigel thinks I should be doing the work of two people."

Felicity hung up. It was obvious that Nigel Lomas had some ulterior motive for bringing her here. Why didn't he want her working cases? Probably because that would take her out of the office and he obviously wanted her to be there as much as possible.

But why?

She didn't have an answer to that question but she was determined to get one.

But first she was going to find out what Linda Dean's ghost was trying to tell her daughter.

The Society might not want her to solve any cases but she was bloody well going to.

16

I called a meeting the following morning at Blackwell Books. If we were going to get into the room beneath the Giza Plateau, the Blackwell sisters were going to have to get us there.

When I arrived at Blackwell Books, Leon, his butler Michael, and Mallory were already there, being served tea at the back of the shop by Devon and Victoria Blackwell.

"Alec," Victoria said when she saw me. "So nice to see you." She pulled me into a brief hug, an action that was repeated by Devon.

"Leon has told us what will be required of us today," Victoria said. "How many people will we be transporting?"

"The four of us," I said, pointing to Mallory, Michael, Leon, and myself. "And Merlin, the two Cabal guys, Carlton, and Amy."

"My, that's a lot of people."

"Is that a problem?"

"The room where we normally perform it won't be able to accommodate everyone."

"We could use the woods," Devon suggested.

Victoria grinned. "Oh, yes, that will be fun! So old-school!"

I didn't say anything. They were in charge of the spell so they could perform it any way they wanted."

"Perhaps we should go totally old-school and cast the spell skyclad," Devon said.

"There's no need for that," I said.

"There's no need for it but it would be fun," Victoria said. "Just like the old days."

The bell above the shop door rang as Carlton entered. He saw us and navigated his way through the jumble of books to get to us. "Hey, boss," he said. "What are we doing here?"

"I told you not to call me that." I introduced him to the witches. They poured him a cup of tea. I declined; I'd tasted enough of the Blackwells' strange brews to last me a lifetime.

Amy came through the door and headed straight to us. "Merlin isn't coming," she said.

"Why not?" It wasn't like him to miss out on the action.

She shrugged. "I don't know. He's been acting

weird. He seems preoccupied, like he's worried about something."

Leon and I exchanged a glance. Merlin's mood had changed when he'd discovered I was enchanted. I had no idea why it would affect him so much but it obviously did. And from what Amy was saying, it sounded like he still hadn't broken out of his funk.

The problem was, I'd counted on him coming along so he could provide some magical muscle if Meyer and Chance tried anything sneaky.

"We don't have to go until later," I said to Amy. "See if you can convince him to come with us before we leave."

"Go where?" she asked.

"We're going to the Pillars of Khonsu."

"But we don't know how to open the gate," Mallory said.

"We don't but the Midnight Cabal does." I told them about our meeting with Tom Meyer and Doug Chance and the deal I'd made with them."

"You didn't have to do that for me," Mallory said.

"Yes, I did."

"Thank you." She drew me into a hug.

"I don't like the sound of this," Amy said. "What if something goes wrong?"

"It won't. We're going to keep an eye on

Meyer and Chance at all times. If they try anything out of line, they're going down."

"Alec," Mallory said. "Maybe they know your mother, since she's a member of the Cabal. They could arrange a meeting."

"Yeah, I've thought of that," I said. "But right now, we need to focus on putting the heart back into Tia's mummy. I can ask them about my mother later, assuming this mission doesn't go sideways."

"Anything you want me to do, boss…I mean Alec?" Carlton asked.

"You're coming with us," I told him.

He raised his hands and shook his head. "No way. I don't go on missions; that isn't in my job description."

I only want you to go as far as the Pillars. When we go through, I want you to place a Janus statue in the gate. That'll make sure it stays open until we come back."

He thought about it for a long while before saying, "Okay, I guess I can do that."

"Amy, I want you to stay with Carlton. Just in case anything goes wrong. I'll feel better knowing there's someone capable on this side of the gate."

Also, I didn't entirely trust Carlton and wanted Amy to keep an eyes on him. I was fairly certain he wasn't a Cabal mole—otherwise he'd have told them where the Pillars were and they wouldn't have had to make a deal with me—but I couldn't put him in charge of our only escape route alone.

"Sure thing," Amy said.

"Great." I turned to the witches. "Where are we going to do this?"

Victoria got a map of Dearmont and unrolled it. She pointed at a spot in the woods just outside of town. This is Frobisher's Glade. It's a picnic area so it's signposted from the highway. There's a lovely clearing there where we can cast the spell."

"A picnic area?" Carlton said. "Sounds too public a place to perform magic. What if there are people there having a picnic?"

Victoria frowned at him. "Not in November, dear."

He nodded. "Point taken."

"So, Mallory, Leon, Michael, and myself will be going through to the realm where Rekhmire lives—or has been imprisoned if you believe the Midnight Cabal. We need to find that mummy as quickly as we can and place the heart inside. Once we've done that, we're out of there. I don't care if Meyer and Chance have found what they're looking for or not. When the curse is lifted, we leave."

"No argument from me," Leon said.

"Okay, so everyone knows what they're doing.

We need to get to the pillar room at around 12:20 so the spell can be cast at twilight, Egyptian time. I told Meyer and Chance to be at my house at 11:30. I'll drive them out to Frobisher's Glade. If you guys could all be at the glade ready to rock, that would be great. We don't know what's on the other side of the gate so bring weapons."

"Are you bringing Excalibur?" Leon asked.

"No," I said without hesitation. The sword might be able to give me a hit of energy but I wasn't sure that was a good thing. Just remembering how good that hit had felt made me realize that it could become addictive very quickly.

"I'll bring a selection of normal and enchanted weapons with me to the woods. We can all choose what we want to take with us before we leave."

I checked my watch. We a bit of time to kill before Meyer and Chance turned up. I needed to call Felicity and see how her new job was going. I didn't want her to think I'd forgotten about her.

"Are there any questions?" I asked the room in general.

"I have a question, sir," Michael said, speaking up for the first time. "Will the teleportation spell work? I seem to remember it can only send people to and from consecrated ground."

"Don't worry about that," Victoria assured

him. "The entire Giza Plateau counts as consecrated ground."

"Anything else?" I asked.

When no one spoke up, I said, "Okay, I'll see you all later. We'll get this curse lifted once and for all."

I left the shop and did a quick mental calculation of time zones. It was almost ten here which meant it would be around three in the afternoon in England. I called Felicity's number. She answered the call immediately.

"Alec! How are you?"

"I'm good," I said. "How are you handling life as a P.I.?"

"It's okay. I've got a case already."

"That's great."

"Yes, it is. Listen, I really can't talk at the moment. Something's come up. I'll ring you back when I have more time, okay?"

"Okay. Sure."

She'd already ended the call.

That wasn't like Felicity at all. I hoped everything was okay.

17

Felicity ducked down below the window in her office. The black van was back, parked across the street in its usual spot. She put her phone back into her pocket. She hated cutting Alec off like that but she had to put a plan she'd been thinking about into motion.

There was an old spell she'd heard of called Clairaudience. After looking it up on the Society database on her laptop, she'd decided she could use it to glean information about the people following her. She had no doubt now that they were members of the Society. Apparently, she'd been brought over to England just so the Society could run surveillance on her. That made absolutely no sense but it was the only conclusion she could come to when she faced the facts.

The spell would let her spy on the occupants of the van. Unfortunately, it would only let her hear what was going on in there and not actually see anything because Clairaudience worked by magically manipulating sound.

She needed to get close to the van because she needed to draw a magical symbol on it to perform the spell. That was going to be difficult. There was no way she could sneak up on the vehicle so she decided to try something a little bolder.

She went downstairs and out through the door that led onto the street. As she walked along the pavement, she reached into her handbag and took out a black marker. Instead of trying to get to the van without being seen—an impossible task since she assumed all eyes in the van were on her—she crossed the road and walked right up to vehicle.

To cover the action of drawing the magical symbol she'd memorized onto the side of the van, she pounded on the passenger door and shouted, "Hello? Is there anyone in there? I know you're following me."

That was all the time it took to draw a small symbol no bigger than a deck of playing cards onto the side of the van.

She quickly retreated to the Ford Focus and got inside. But instead of starting the engine, she used the marker to draw an identical symbol to the one she'd put on the van on the car's radio. She chanted the words of the spell, which she'd written on a scrap of paper, and turned the radio on.

Instead of music, what came out of the speakers were two voices, a man's and a woman's.

"Why the hell was she banging like that?" he said.

"I don't know," the woman replied. "I told you she was bound to notice us if we parked in the same bloody spot every time."

"It's a big van. I can't park it just anywhere can I? There has to be enough room."

"Ha," she scoffed. "You men always think things are bigger than they actually are."

There was a momentary silence and then the man said, "What do you think she's doing just sitting in her car like that?"

"How the hell should I know?"

"Maybe she's arranged to make contact with him in the car. He might turn up in a minute. Keep your eyes peeled."

"I hope he turns up soon. I'm sick of this stakeout crap. It isn't anything like how it looks in the movies. It's bloody boring."

"She's boring, you mean," he said.

"Who? Felicity?"

"Who else? Have we been watching someone else I don't know about?"

"All right," the woman said. "No need to be like that. Remember, Felicity is the key to finding the target. She might be boring but she has her uses."

Felicity frowned at the radio. What the hell was that supposed to mean? The key to finding what target?"

"Sssh," the man said. "They're calling for a situation report." His voice became a little more formal and it was obvious he was speaking to someone on a phone. 'All normal here. No contact has been made between Lake and the target yet. There's no sign of the target at all."

"Well they're not very happy," he said.

"Of course they're not," she replied. "This whole operation is a huge waste of time."

"We can't say that."

"Can't we? We've been on her since day one and we've seen neither hair nor hide of the target."

"He'll come. The prophecy, remember."

"Well maybe prophecies can be wrong."

"I doubt it," he said. "Have you ever known a prophecy to be wrong?"

"There's a first time for everything. And knowing our bloody luck, this will be that time."

The voices coming out of the radio faded for a

second and were replaced with a static hiss. The spell was wearing off.

"He'll show," the man's voice came faintly through the hiss. "He has to."

The voices died and the radio began playing music.

Felicity felt a lump in her throat. She hadn't really been promoted to P.I. at all. She'd been brought here as bait. Whomever the target was that the people in the van had been talking about, they seemed sure he'd meet Felicity here because of some prophecy.

She felt a hot tear slide down her cheek. Why had she been stupid enough to believe she could be a P.I.? All she was good for was being used as a pawn in some stupid game the Society was playing.

She looked at the door with her name on it and felt like going over there and smashing the glass into a thousand shards. It was a sham, all of it. The office, the tattoos, the case. All a sham.

No, not the case. That was real.

Whether she was actually a P.I. or not, Felicity was going to help Jessica Baker. She was going to find out what Linda Dean was trying to communicate and right the wrongs that had been done to her.

18

Meyer and Chance arrived at my house at exactly 11:30. I went outside and ushered them into the Land Rover. As they climbed inside, I realized there was something missing, something wrong. It wasn't until we hit Main Street that I realized what it was; they had no bags. For people who intended to loot a temple, pyramid or whatever the hell Rekhmire lived in, they were totally unprepared.

"So, what are you guys hoping to find today?" I asked them.

Meyer, who was sitting in the front seat next to me, shrugged. "We'll see what's there when we get there."

I nodded but didn't say anything. I found it hard to believe that their plan could be so nonchalant.

"You still haven't told us how we're getting there," Chance said from the backseat.

"Magic," I told him.

He chuckled.

"What's so funny?"

"You Society people. You act like you want magic to be eradicated but you use it yourselves all the time."

"We don't want magic to be eradicated."

"Is that why you keep its existence a secret from the general public?"

"No, we do that to make sure they aren't scared out of their minds."

He shook his head. "You're hypocrites."

"Hey, at least we don't want to destroy the world."

"We don't want to destroy the world either," he said.

"You want to unleash all the monsters from the shadows and let them roam free. You want everyone to live in terror. That sounds like the destruction of the world to me."

"You two, quit it," Meyer said.

We drove in silence the rest of the way.

The sign for Frobisher's Glade took us off the highway and along a narrow road that wound into the woods. After ten minutes, we reached a parking lot and a clearing that was full of picnic tables. The Blackwells had marked out a magical circle on the grass and were standing next to it with Mallory, Amy, Carlton, Leon, and Michael. A small altar had been placed near the circle and a fire burned in a large brazier, sending white smoke up into the cold November air.

I was disappointed that Merlin wasn't here. Whatever his problem was, he still hadn't gotten over it.

The Blackwell sisters had opted not to perform the ritual skyclad. Instead of their usual black lace dresses, though, they wore long white robes which reached down to their feet and seemed to be made of satin.

I parked next to Mallory's Blazer and got out.

While Meyer and Chance wandered away to speak to each other in private, I opened the Land Rover's tailgate, revealing a collection of weapons. I also had the Janus statue and the Box of Midnight, which contained the remains of Tia's heart.

The others came over and helped themselves to weapons. Leon, Michael, Mallory, and myself —the four of us who would be going through the gate—each had a sword. Mallory and I also had a dagger each. Leon and Michael had brought shotguns. Amy had her service weapon. Carlton was unarmed so he carried the Janus statue and the Box of Midnight.

We walked across the grass to the circle.

Meyer and Chance were still deep in conversation.

"Hey," I shouted at them. "Are you coming?"

They both nodded and walked toward the circle.

"I don't like this," Leon said. "They're definitely plotting something."

"Keep your eye on them. There's no way they're going through that gate just to loot the place. They have something else in mind."

Meyer and Chance stepped into the circle. I shivered slightly and it wasn't only because of the November chill.

"Are we ready to begin?" Victoria asked.

"Before we go," I said. "We need to discuss bringing us back. The room is underground so we won't be able to call you."

"Oh," she said. "What do you want us to do then?"

"Give us two hours. After that time, bring us back."

She nodded. "All right. But we can only bring you back from the room we're sending you to. So make sure you're all in that room within two hours. Now, shall we begin?"

Everyone nodded but no one spoke. A solemnity had descended over all of us.

Devon Blackwell took a silver bowl from the altar and came forward with it, along with eight ritual daggers. She handed a dagger to each of us and held out the bowl. "A drop of blood from each of you, please."

I cut my finger and let the blood drip into the bowl, which contained herbs and leaves. Devon moved from one person to the next collecting the blood. Victoria took the daggers from us and the two witches returned to the altar.

They began chanting in strange languages that had creeped me out every time I'd heard them in the past and did so now.

The perimeter of the circle began to spark with energy. The sisters increased the pace of their words and I felt the energy move inward, filling the circle. It felt as if it were spinning, gaining speed and power. The hairs on the back of my neck stood on end. The world beyond the circle seemed to shimmer.

Devon moved to the brazier, the silver bowl in her hands.

The words the two women spoke mingled and twisted together.

Devon tipped the contents of the bowl into the brazier. The white smoke turned red.

The world beyond the circle vanished and was replaced in an instant. We were no longer standing in Frobisher's Glade; now we were inside a large room whose walls were made of huge sandy colored stone blocks. The ceiling was at least twenty feet high. A wide set of stone steps led up to a dais. Standing upon the dais, the Pillars of Khonsu waited.

They looked just like Tia's drawing.

I tightened my grip on my sword. Meyer and Chance had gotten what they needed from us. If they planned to take us out and go through the gate alone, now would be the time to strike.

But they didn't do that. They both ascended the steps to the pillars. Chance checked his watch. He looked at Meyer and said, "It is time."

They began chanting and drawing magical shapes in the air with their fingers.

I turned to Carlton. "When the gate opens, place the Janus statue halfway into it. That will prevent it from closing until we're back."

He nodded solemnly and gave the Box of Midnight to Mallory.

The two Cabal members were still chanting and now I could see a blue light emanating from the space between the pillars. "Come on," I said to the others. I ascended the steps with Leon, Michael, and Mallory. Carlton and Amy hung back.

Meyer and Chance seemed to have completed their spell. Between the pillars, a bright blue square of crackling energy had appeared.

"That's it," Meyer said. "That's the gate. We

simply step through and we will be in the realm where Rekhmire is imprisoned."

"After you," I said, gesturing to the blue portal.

He nodded, stepped into the blue sparks, and disappeared. I followed him. As I stepped forward, the energy overwhelmed my senses for a split second and then I was suddenly underwater. The dark liquid was cold against my skin and I couldn't see anything. I didn't even know how far it was to the surface.

Kicking my legs, I swam upward and broke the surface. I breathed in a deep lungful of air to find it tasted slightly sulfurous. I was in a square man-made pool that was ringed with large flagstones. At one end of the pool, a huge stone structure rose into the air. Its shape was that of a pyramidal stepped temple.

Beyond the pool and the structure, red desert sands stretched as far as the eye could see. The sky was also tinged red with billowing clouds of purple in the distance.

I swam to the edge of the pool.

Meyer was standing on the flagstones, staring at the building. "Beautiful, isn't it?"

That was one word for it, I supposed. But where he saw beauty, I saw danger. We had no idea what was in there.

Mallory surfaced in the pool and I took the

box from her as she climbed out. Leon was next, then Michael, followed by Chance.

When the six of us were all standing on the flagstones, we checked our weapons and prepared ourselves for whatever might lie ahead.

There was no entrance into the structure at ground level. Near the apex, hundreds of feet up from where we stood, a square doorway had been cut into the stone.

"Looks like we have some climbing to do," I said.

Because the sides of the temple were stepped, we didn't have to actually climb but it was going to be a tough ascent. I just hoped that nothing was waiting in that doorway to kill us when we arrived up there with aching legs and our energy depleted.

We walked to the base of the structure and began our ascent. As we went up, I asked Mallory how she was feeling.

"Fine," she said. "Why?"

"I know how Tia reacts whenever Rekhmire is mentioned. Now that we're here where he lives, I thought she might be seething with emotion."

Mallory shook her head. "No, she's gone quiet."

I wasn't sure if that was good or bad.

We kept going. The muscles in my legs were feeling solid now and I knew that soon they'd be full of lactic acid and cramping up. I looked over at Meyer and Chance. If they were planning anything underhanded, that plan had probably been overridden by the pain they were feeling. They both had their heads down and were covered in sweat.

Leon and Michael were powering through it, marching up the steep steps with determined looks in their eyes.

"How are you guys doing?" I asked them.

"No problem, sir," Michael said.

"How about you, Leon?"

"The air smells of farts," he said.

That lightened the mood. Even Meyer and Chance chuckled.

When we finally got to the top, we were out of breath, sweaty, and aching. Luckily, nothing came out of the doorway and tried to eat us.

After I got my breath back, I went to the doorway and peered inside. A set of steps led down, curving out of sight.

"Everyone ready?" I asked. The others got behind me and I descended, sword ready in case anything should come rushing up the steps toward me. The stairs took us to a large stone-floored room that was lit with flaming torches on the walls. Statues of jackal-headed warriors stood beneath the torches. Each was dressed in gold mail and held a kopesh—a sword with a sickle-like blade—in its hand.

"This isn't creepy at all," Leon said sarcastically.

At the far end of the room, another set of steps led down into the bowels of the structure.

Cautiously, we advanced across the room. I'd seen enough movies to know what was going to happen next. "Those statues are going to come to life aren't they?" I whispered.

When we were exactly halfway across the room, the flagstone beneath my feet clicked as I stepped on it. "I've triggered a trap," I told the others.

The jackal-headed guards began to move, advancing toward us, their swords gleaming in the light from the wall torches.

"Yeah," I said. "I knew the statues would come to life."

19

Felicity got to the cemetery at eight and parked the Focus in the empty car park outside the gate. The night was cold. She was wrapped up in a padded jacket, beanie, and gloves but she still felt the bite of the frosty air through her clothing. Her breath clouded in front of her face.

She pushed on the gate and it opened. Charlie had been true to his word. Felicity slipped inside and closed the gate behind her.

Away from the streetlights, the cemetery was lit only by moonlight. Felicity stood with her back to the gate for a few seconds, waiting for her eyes to adjust to the difference in light values. The headstones seemed bleached in the moonlight, like rows of gray bones.

She followed the path to the point where Jessica had taken her and then walked across the grass between the graves, looking for the headstone that bore Linda Dean's name. She knew it was by the trees somewhere but the cemetery looked different at nighttime and she had to search for almost twenty minutes before she finally found Linda's grave.

She wasn't sure what to do now she was here. Just wait around she supposed. She wished she had an EMF meter. At least then she could check the grave for abnormal readings. But she didn't have such a device so she just had to stand here in the cold.

Welcome to the life of a P.I.

But she wasn't a P.I. Not really. She'd given her life to the Society of Shadows and they repaid her by giving her a false promotion so they could catch some target. Most of what she'd heard in the van hadn't even made sense. Why would they set her up as bait? Who would try to make contact with her? She didn't really know many people in England anymore. Not people the Society would be interested in, anyway.

Once this case was solved, she was going to resign. There was no point in working for an organization that treated you this badly. She'd loved working for the Society once. It had been her entire life. But the organization had become splintered by politics. There were factions within factions. Spies. Traitors. Half of the Society seemed to be made up of Cabal members these days.

She sighed and wrapped her arms around herself to keep warm. This ghost had better turn up soon or she'd freeze to death.

Something pale stepped out from the trees. Felicity took a step back. She felt suddenly silly for not asking Jessica to show her a photo of her mother. How would she recognize the ghost? Then she felt silly for having that thought. How many ghosts could there be in this cemetery?

The figure that stepped out in front of her was partially wrapped a shroud. Felicity looked at the face and found that of a woman in her sixties.

"Linda," Felicity said, steeling herself even though her heart was fluttering like a butterfly trapped in a jar. "Do you have something to tell me?"

Linda raised one arm and pointed at the perimeter wall.

This was the same action Jessica had described seeing in her bedroom.

"What are you trying to show me?" Felicity asked, stepping forward and letting her gaze follow the ghost's pointing finger. There was nothing there except trees, the wall, and shadows.

Why would Linda try to show Felicity something in the cemetery and try to show Jessica something through her bedroom window?

Unless the same thing could be seen at both locations, it didn't make sense.

"You're not pointing at something are you?" she said to the ghost. "You're pointing in a direction. Do you want me to follow you?"

The ghost didn't reply but merely flickered out of existence for a split second. She reappeared by the wall. She pointed in the same direction, only now, her hand disappeared into the bricks of the wall.

"All right," Felicity said. She obviously had to leave the cemetery because Linda was pointing in a direction beyond the wall. She went back to the path and followed it to the gate, which she opened and slipped through, remembering to close it behind her as she'd promised Charlie.

The ghost was on the street now, beneath one of the streetlights, waiting.

Felicity walked toward Linda. Again, the ghost flickered out of existence and then reappeared farther along the street. Felicity wasn't sure if she should follow on foot or in her car.

Deciding to try the car, she got in to the Focus and drove along the road toward Linda. The ghost moved forward at a rapid, flickering speed, constantly disappearing and reappearing farther along the road.

Felicity followed.

When they came to crossroads, the ghost flickered left. Felicity turned left.

Ten minutes later, during which time the ghost had taken Felicity through parts of town that were busy even at this time of night, they arrived at an empty gravel car park by the canal.

Felicity got out of the car. She was certain no that only she could see Linda's ghost. They'd traveled through some parts of town where there were people walking along the pavement in the areas where Linda had flickered in and out of existence. None of those people had seen her.

Whether that meant Linda had chosen to reveal herself to Felicity—as she'd chosen to reveal herself to her daughter—or just that Felicity was sensitive to this sort of thing, she had no idea. All she knew was that a ghost had led her across Manchester to the canal in which her body had been found.

Felicity knew that this must be the place where Linda had been killed.

She looked at the ghost and said, "Show me."

Linda turned toward the canal. She didn't flicker this time; she floated toward the bank.

Felicity left the car park and made her way over the grass to the water's edge. This area was overgrown and the grass reached up to her knees. The ghost had stopped and was pointing at the ground a couple of feet from where Felicity stood.

Crouching down and carefully brushing the grass aside, Felicity saw something glimmer in the moonlight. She didn't touch it. Instead, she took her phone from her pocket and used its light to confirm her suspicions.

Lying in the grass was a silver heart-shaped necklace with a broken chain. Felicity could see the engraving on the metal. LD.

Linda Dean.

"I couldn't show this to Jessica." The voice made Felicity jump. She turned to face Linda's ghost. "I couldn't show Jessica," the ghost repeated. "This would be too upsetting for her. I can show you."

Swallowing back tears she felt suddenly threaten, Felicity nodded. "Yes, you can show me. I'll make it right."

She stood up and checked the area. She needed to get the police her somehow, needed them to find this locket. Then they could examine the crime scene and get one step closer to finding Linda's killer.

She spotted something in the car park that made her heart skip a beat. A CCTV camera mounted on a pole. It's function was obviously to monitor the parked cars but it looked like the view from its lens might extend to this patch of grass as well.

Felicity went back to the car and turned on the GPS. She got the location of the car park and called the police. She left no name and simply told them that the detectives investigating the murder of Linda Dean should investigate the patch of grass by the car park. She gave them the exact location and ended the call.

As she drove away from the area, she looked in the rearview mirror and saw the ghost of Linda Dean watching her from the canal bank.

Linda raised a hand briefly in a wave of thanks.

20

I raised my sword to ward off the kopesh that was slicing through the air toward my skull. Steel clashed with steel and sparks flew. The same ring of steel on steel filled the room as each of us fought for survival against the jackal headed temple guards.

Just as I deflected the attack from above, another came from the side. I dived out of the way of the arcing blade. The stone floor rushed up to meet me and I angled my body so that my momentum sent me rolling away from my attackers.

Springing to my feet, I hacked at a guard that was attacking Michael. My sword dug into its shoulder and as I pulled it free, Michael delivered a fatal blow to the creature's neck with his own sword.

"Thank you, sir," he said, bringing up the barrel of his shotgun and dispatching a guard with a blast right between the eyes.

My two attackers caught up with me. They struck at the same time, one from the left, the other from the right. I deflected the blow from my left with my blade, a move that resulted in a loud clang as the two swords met and a shower of sparks that scattered away like crazy fireflies.

The attack from my right sliced through my shirt but I managed to angle my body so that it was otherwise harmless. As I pirouetted, I drove the point of my sword into the guard on my left.

The one on the right was still moving forward with the momentum of its swinging sword. I smashed my elbow into its snout and while it was still reeling, I advanced and sliced the edge of my blade into its neck.

With both of my attackers dealt with, I looked at the fray around me to see if anyone needed my help.

Mallory was fighting off one of the guards but I saw she had things well in hand as she thrust forward like a fencer and pierced the creature's chest. It went down like a sack of rocks.

Michael was blasting away with his shotgun and had already taken down five of the guards as far as I could see.

Leon was taking on two of them so I evened

the odds by killing one of them for him. He thanked me and drove his sword into the eye of the other.

I looked around the room. The jackal guards were all dead.

Meyer and Chance seemed to know how to handle themselves. It looked like they'd killed six between them.

The air was filled with the coppery tang of blood.

We moved quickly across the room to the steps that led deeper into the pyramid. After triggering the trap in the jackal room, I moved more cautiously. It took us a while to get to the next room because of that and because we had descended a long way. In fact, I guessed the we might actually be underground.

The steps terminated at a doorway that was bordered with gold edging etched with hieroglyphs. Whatever was beyond this door was probably important. Keeping my sword ready, I advanced through the doorway carefully.

The room beyond was huge. We had to be underground because a room of these dimensions wouldn't have fitted inside the pyramidal structure above ground.

The room was oblong in shape and had been fashioned so that one half was about five feet higher than the other. The lower floor was littered with statues, canopic jars, furniture, and sarcophagi. The upper floor was bare but on the wall there was what looked like a lens with dark red mist swirling behind it. The lens was surrounded by a border of gold that had been etched with hieroglyphs like the door I'd just passed through but in a much larger scale.

"That's the prison," Meyer said. "Rekhmire is trapped behind it."

"And here's all the treasure you could want," I said, indicating the chaotic arrangement of items in the lower floor.

I turned to Mallory. "Tia's mummy must be in one of the sarcophagi. Do you know which one?"

She shook her head. "I have no idea but she might know."

"Okay, can you ask her or whatever it is you do?"

She nodded. "I'll have to let her out."

I nodded. She dropped the upper part of her body forward. Her hair covered her face.

The sound of clattering armor and weapons came from the stairs we'd just descended. Leon turned in that direction. "Shit, we've got company."

"Can you hold them off?" I asked him.

He grinned. "Of course. Michael, let's go." They both disappeared through the gold-edged door and up the stairs.

I turned my attention back to Mallory. She was breathing hard, her ribcage expanding and contracting rapidly. She lifted her face and I saw the hieroglyphs beneath her skin and the black eyes.

"It is here," she said, her voice sounding like a needle scratching over parchment. "My body. It is here.'

I indicated the sarcophagi. "Can you find it among all of this?"

She nodded and stepped forward, trailing her hieroglyph-covered hand over the sarcophagi as she passed them. I followed closely.

"Somewhere here," she whispered. "This way." She led me between the piles of riches and artifacts, stopping to touch each sarcophagus. Her mummy seemed to have been squirreled away somewhere. We'd already walked the length of a football field and there were plenty of areas we hadn't explored yet.

"Over here," she said, increasing her pace. She went over to a sarcophagus that was leaning upright against the wall. The box was decorated with gold and paints to represent a beautiful woman. "This," she said, pointing at it and looking at me. "This is my body."

She was holding the Box of Midnight, clutching it to her chest. "Mallory must replace the heart." Her head fell forward.

While she was bringing Mallory back, I removed the sarcophagus's lid and set it aside. Inside, Tia's mummified body was wrapped in linen.

"Alec, it's time," Mallory said from behind me.

I stepped aside. She reached for the linen swaddling that covered the mummy's chest and tore at it, revealing the dead, blackened skin beneath. Mallory pulled at the linen some more, uncovering a hole in the chest cavity. This was where Tia's heart had been before Rekhmire had ripped it out. Now, we were going to reverse that wicked deed.

Mallory opened the box and took out the blackened, shriveled heart. Holding it in her right hand, she placed it back inside the mummified body. This was what Felicity had seen in an ancient image and had realized was the way to lift the curse. I wished she could have been here to see this. It wouldn't have been possible without her.

"Nothing's happening," Mallory said. Then her eyes opened wide and she gasped. "The heart just beat in my hand."

"It's working," I said.

She smiled and tears sprang from her eyes, rolling down her cheeks as she let out a laugh. "I can feel the heart reconnecting to Tia." She removed her hand and stepped back.

We both watched as the shriveled form beneath the linen filled out, stretching the fabric. The exposed hole in the chest began to close and the skin that had been dead only moments before now became living tissue.

Tia stepped out of the sarcophagus and ripped the linen coverings from her body. Her naked body was covered with tattooed hieroglyph that were probably an ancient version of my own magical tattoos.

"We did it," Mallory said. "We actually did it."

Tia nodded and smiled at her. "The curse is lifted, Mallory." Her voice didn't sound like a papyrus scratch anymore; now, it was rich and melodic.

She turned in the direction we'd come and pointed at the raised part of the floor where Rekhmire's prison was located. Meyer and Chance were up there, reading the hieroglyphs on the gold rim of the lens. They were so far away, it was difficult to know exactly what they were doing.

Tia looked at me and said, "They are breaking the seal. They are releasing Rekhmire."

21

Felicity woke up disorientated, wondering where she was. It took her a couple of minutes to realize she wasn't in Maine anymore and that the bedroom she was looking at was her new bedroom in Manchester.

Sunlight was streaming in through the curtains. She must have overslept. The clock on the bedside table told her that she had indeed overslept. It was almost lunchtime.

She slid out of bed and went downstairs to the kitchen. Maybe a cup of tea would wake her up. She put the kettle on and sat at the kitchen table while she waited for it to boil. Her phone was on the table so she picked it up and checked it out of habit. She had three missed calls from Jessica Baker.

She decided to ring Jessica back after she'd had a cup of tea. She had plenty to tell her.

While she was pouring the boiled water into a teapot, the phone rang. It was Jessica again. Felicity answered it.

"You did it," Jessica said before Felicity even had a chance to say hello. "I can't believe it. You've seen the News, right?"

"No," Felicity said. "What's happened?"

"Put BBC News on right now."

She went into the living room, found the remote and turned the TV on. After some wrangling with the remote, she found BBC News.

Behind the female news presenter was an inset image showing a white police tent that had been set up on the canal bank. Uniformed officers and forensic scientists were going about their work. Felicity recognized the location; she'd been there last night.

"*...was arrested this morning after an anonymous tip led police to the location by the canal in Manchester,*" the presenter was saying. "*The police, who had no leads up to this point found evidence that this was the place where Linda Dean was murdered. A CCTV camera at a nearby car park had captured an image of the killer's car. This led to the arrest of Mr Dugan. Police are also questioning him regarding three other similar murders in the area.*"

"Did my mother show you that place?" Jessica asked. "Did you call the police?"

"Yes," Felicity said.

"I knew it. She came to me last night while I was in bed. But she wasn't distraught or pointing or anything like that. She just sat on the bed and stroked my hair until I fell asleep. I think she was saying goodbye."

"She probably was," Felicity said.

"I can't thank you enough," Jessica said. "Make sure you send me an invoice for your services."

"There won't be any invoice," Felicity told her. "I'm just glad I could help."

"Thank you again. I have to go, there are reporters on our lawn and Rob's getting mad with them."

"Okay, bye, Jessica." She hung up and decided that she'd place some flowers on Linda Dean's grave today. It only seemed right since Linda had helped her solve her first and only case. After she'd done that, she'd ring Nigel Lomas and tell him where to stick his fake P.I. job. If he wanted bait to attract a "target" he was going to have to get someone else to do it.

She showered, dressed in warm clothes, and drove to a local florist where she bought a spray of pink peonies. She also bought a small rose that she intended to give to Charlie Sutherland to thank him for his help. He seemed to like flowers and the rose—which was a lovely vibrant yellow —would look nice wherever he chose to plant it.

She got to the cemetery in the early afternoon. The sun was bright in the sky but the November chill was still in the air and she made sure to don her hat and gloves before going through the open gates. The cemetery office was open today and through the glass in the door, she could see two female employees hard at work.

As she followed the gravel path among the headstones, she looked for Charlie but couldn't see him. It would be just her luck to buy him a present on his day off. She went to Linda Dean's grave and placed the peonies in a plastic vase that was standing by the headstone. "I hope you find peace now," she said, touching the headstone gently.

She looked around for Charlie again but it was obvious that he wasn't here today. Perhaps she'd have to come back tomorrow. On her way out, with the yellow rose still in her hand, she decided to ask in the office when Charlie would be back. They'd probably know his shifts.

She pushed through the door and was greeted with friendly smiles from the two ladies in the office. "Hello, how can I help you?" one of them asked.

"I was just wondering if you know when Charlie Sutherland will be back on duty."

The woman frowned. "Charlie Sutherland? I haven't heard that name in a while, have you, Karen?"

"No," Karen said from her desk.

"I don't understand," Felicity said. "What do you mean?"

"Charlie used to work here but it was well before our time," Karen said. "We hear his name every now and then though when people ask about him. They think they've seen him. Some even think they've spoken to him. He's one of our local ghosts if you believe in that sort of thing." She chuckled.

"Oh," Felicity said, taken aback. She wasn't sure what to say or do. "I bought this rose for him."

"Aah, that's nice," the woman who'd first spoken to her said. "Well you can give it to him. His grave is at the back of the cemetery." She produced a map of the plots and pointed out where Felicity was to go.

Felicity barely understood what she was being told. Her mind was racing. Charlie was a ghost. Did Jessica know that it was a ghost she'd spoken to after her father's death? That a ghost had helped her?

If not, Felicity saw no reason to enlighten her. She thanked the office staff and went back outside into the cold sunlight. She walked the path again, this time all the way to the rear of the cemetery. A short trek over the grass brought her to an overgrown grave whose headstone bore the name Charlie Sutherland. He'd died in 1942. Felicity checked the surrounding stones but couldn't see any other Sutherlands. Perhaps that was why he hadn't moved on; he had no one waiting for him on the other side. So he'd chosen to stay here and help people who were grieving.

Using her hand, she dug a small hole in the grave and planted the yellow rose in it. She stood up and smiled at her memory of the friendly old man who'd spoken to her and even opened the cemetery gates for her. "Thank you, Charlie," she said.

She walked back along the path to the gates and turned to take one last look at the place before she left.

Standing by his grave at the back of the cemetery, she saw Charlie. He was standing there watching her. When he realized she'd noticed him, he touched the brim of his tweed cap and grinned

Felicity waved to him and left.

22

"We have to stop them!" I shouted, running back between the rows of treasure to the magical prison.

Mallory joined me. Together, we sprinted toward Meyer and Chance.

Until we both became frozen mid-stride. All of my muscles had become like blocks of granite. Even though I only had one foot on the ground, I didn't fall over because I was being suspended in the air by some sort of magic. Mallory was in the same position, frozen in a running position and hanging in the air by some unseen force.

"I cannot let you stop them," Tia said, walking between us. "I must have my revenge on Rekhmire. I cannot do that while is locked away behind a magical door like a coward."

I tried to speak, to plead with her to stop

Meyer and Chance, but my mouth was as immobile as the rest of my body.

"Once they have opened the prison, I will kill them if you wish," Tia said. "But at the moment, they are of more use to me alive than dead."

I couldn't let them release Rekhmire. I had to get out of this binding spell. My mind raced for a solution but nothing presented itself.

Tia walked away from us and stepped up onto the raised floor by the prison. The dark red smoke behind the lens swirled in a clockwise circle, first slowly and then faster while Meyer and Chance spoke strange words and drew mystical patterns in the air.

Tia simply watched them, waiting for her arch enemy to emerge from the red smoke.

I had to do something. A magic circle materialized in my thoughts. This had happened to me before and it usually meant I was able to tap into the enchantment that had been engraved on my bones. In the past, I'd been able to cast an energy ball, raise a magical shield, and heal. The magic circles for those abilities had been blue, green, and red respectively.

The circle that presented itself to me now was black. It was also the most complex of the circles I'd seen, made up of Enochian letters, Egyptian hieroglyphs, runes, a pentagram and a unicursal hexagram combined, along with other symbols I didn't recognize.

I knew that if I concentrated on the symbol, some sort of power would be raised. I also knew that it would knock seven kinds of hell out of me afterward. I'd collapse from exhaustion and probably black out. Could I risk that here in Rekhmire's lair?

Did I have a choice?

I concentrated on the black symbol.

As soon as I directed my attention to the symbol, I felt the spell that was holding me begin to weaken. Limited movement came back to my limbs and my bodyweight brought me closer to the ground as the unseen force that suspended me in the air began to fail.

I concentrated harder on the symbol.

Tia's spell broke. Mallory and I fell to the floor. As I got up I noticed that our swords, which should be glowing blue because they were enchanted, had lost their magic. Their glow was gone, the blades now simple steel.

"What was that?" Mallory asked, getting to her feet.

"I don't know. Some kind of anti-magic. We can worry about it later. Right now, we have to make sure Rekhmire stays in his prison."

We ran forward. Tia saw us and her brow creased with confusion. She raised her hands, ready to cast another spell, but the red smoke suddenly spilled out from the lens, obscuring everything in the room.

"We're too late," Mallory said.

A figure stepped from the prison. He was at least seven feet tall, wrapped in linen, the same as the bindings that had been around Tia's mummy. Rekhmire's linen ended at the neck, though, exposing his face. It was virtually a skull with thin skin stretched over it like parchment. From within the deep eye sockets stared two yellow eyes with red irises. The only adornment he wore was a scarab beetle made of blue stone. It hung around his neck on a leather cord.

"Rekhmire!" Tia shouted. "You will pay for what you did to me!" She leapt at him, hands glowing with a luminescent green light.

He raised his own hands to ward her off. His glowed dark red, the same as the smoke that had come out of the lens and was now dissipating.

They tussled. Meyer and Chance stepped out of the way.

"Lord Rekhmire," Meyer said, "Don't waste you power on this woman."

Still fighting Tia, Rekhmire looked at Meyer and said, "Don't tell me what to do." He raised one hand and shot a red bolt at Meyer. The Cabal member went crashing into the pile of antiquities. Judging by the force that had pushed him and the distance he'd traveled, I doubted he was still alive.

Seeing what had happened to his partner, Chance hunkered down into a child's pose and kept his mouth shut.

The blue glow on our swords was slowly returning. They flickered like faulty light bulbs before finally reaching full illumination. So the anti-magic blast had a limited lifespan. Good to know. I didn't want to inadvertently deactivate all my enchanted weapons.

Returning his attention to the sorceress, Rekhmire used one hand to grab her neck and lift her off her feet. He brought back his other hand as if he were about to plunge it into her stomach. His fist glowed with crimson power that rose from it like oily smoke.

"I see you have your heart back," he sneered. "I'll just have to rip it out of you again."

Suddenly, Mallory was leaping through the air. I hadn't even noticed her leave my side. She brought her sword down in an overhead chop. It sliced through the arm that was holding Tia.

Both the sorceress and the severed arm fell to the floor.

Rekhmire howled and used his good hand to hold the stump that now protruded from his left shoulder. For a moment, he was distracted by his pain. This was our only chance to get out of here alive.

I rushed forward and grabbed Tia, hefting her over my shoulder and making for the gold-edged door. Mallory stayed close behind me. "Go ahead," I told her. "Tell Leon and Michael we have to get out of here now. They need to clear a path to the exit."

She ran ahead up the stairs.

With the weight of Tia on my shoulder, I had a long climb ahead.

Doug Chance appeared behind me. "You were going to leave me!" he moaned.

"Yeah, I was," I told him truthfully. "You didn't come here to loot the temple; you came to release Rekhmire. Anything that happens after that is on you."

"We were going to make a pact with him," he said. "Have him join our cause. With him at the head of the Midnight Cabal, we'd be unstoppable. I hadn't counted on that stupid bitch ruining everything."

"Unless you want me to throw you back down those stairs, shut the hell up," I said. "This woman suffered at his hands. Can you blame her for wanting revenge?" Okay, Tia's timing sucked but I wasn't going to tell Chance that.

He went quiet. As we climbed the stairs, we had to step over and around dead bodies. Most of them were jackal guards like the ones we'd fought in the room above but there was also some sort of demon dog and a weird thing that had membranous wings like a bat.

It must have taken thirty grueling minutes to get up the steps and into the room where we'd first fought the jackal guards. Leon, Michael, and Mallory were waiting for us there.

We ascended the shorter flight of stairs to the doorway and descended the side of the pyramidal structure.

"Would you like me to take the lady, sir?" Michael asked.

"Thanks, Michael." I passed Tia over to him. He was probably a lot stronger than me and he carried her as if her weight was nothing.

Going down the steps was just as bad as going up them. An insidious weakness began to creep up on me and I knew it was because of the anti-magic spell I'd cast earlier. If it was going to drain me the same as the other spells did, I was probably going to pass out at some point.

We finally made it to ground level and together, we plunged into the pool. In the inky water, I saw a blue glow in the depths and swam toward it.

The next thing I knew I was being deposited roughly on the stone floor in the pillar room. I looked around to check that everyone had made it through. We were all here but maybe we weren't all okay.

Tia was lying on the floor on her back where Michael had placed her. Mallory was sitting next to her, crying.

I went over and checked for a pulse in Tia's neck.

There was nothing.

At some point during the journey back, she'd died. Rekhmire had killed her after all.

"I'm sorry," I said to Mallory. "I know she was your friend."

"She was more than that," she said through the tears. "All that time we spent together in Shadow Land, we became like sisters. We relied on each other, trusted each other, helped each other. I can't believe she's gone."

She stroked the sorceress's black hair and cried quietly.

"Carlton," I said. "You can remove the Janus statue now."

He did so and the portal vanished. The Pillars of Khonsu were just ordinary pillars again and between them, where there had been a portal to another dimension, there was now only the dusty air of the room.

I checked my watch. Thanks to the grueling climbs involved, we'd only just made it back within the two hour deadline.

A sudden gasp came from Tia's body. She sat up, her eyes wide.

"You're alive!" Mallory said.

The sorceress nodded and stroked Mallory's hair. "Yes, of course. I am kept alive by magic. Rekhmire would have killed me if he had taken my heart but you prevented him from doing that. Thank you."

"I'm sorry you didn't get the revenge you wanted," Mallory said.

"Something tells me you'll get another chance," I said to Tia. "I don't think that's the last we've seen of him, especially if the Cabal has its way." I shot a look at Chance.

He merely shrugged. The Cabal knew where the Pillars of Khonsu were located now and they had the spell that opened the portal. There was no way they'd just leave a powerful being like Rekhmire in another realm. I had absolutely no doubt that they'd try to recruit him into their nefarious organization.

The temple room vanished and suddenly we were all in Frobisher's Glade. The cold air bit my skin, reviving me a little from the lethargy I felt.

"Who wants to join me for a drink?" Leon said. "I'm buying."

He had a number of takers, even the Blackwell sisters. Only Chance and I declined. I had to get home because I knew I was going to be suffering from exhaustion pretty soon and he had to go back to whatever rock he'd crawled out from under.

I drove him back to my place where his car was parked. We rode in silence all the way. He was probably what a win for the Cabal today was. Rekhmire was released from his prison and they knew how to get to him. I was thinking what a win today was for Mallory. The curse was lifted.

I should probably call Felicity and tell her all about it but after the last call, I figured she was pretty busy. She said she'd call me so I'd respect that and wait until she was ready.

When we got out of the Land Rover outside my house and Chance was about to get into his own car, I said, "Hey, before you go. Do you know my mother."

He chuckled to himself. "I know *of* her."

"She's pretty high up in the Cabal, is that right?"

He scoffed. "Not since we found out what she really is." He opened his car door and slid inside.

"What do you mean by that?" I asked.

His window buzzed down. "You mean you don't know? Wow, not only was she lying to us for all those years, she was lying to her own son too." He laughed and drove off, leaving me bewildered on the sidewalk.

I went inside and felt a sudden drop in my

energy level. So sudden that I had to lean against the wall to make sure I didn't fall over.

There was a knock on the door. Maybe it was Chance coming back to explain what he'd meant about my mother. I opened the door. It was Merlin.

"Go away," I groaned. "I need sleep."

He stepped inside and took me by the shoulder, leading me into the living room. "It isn't sleep you need, Alec. You need something much more potent."

I dropped onto the sofa and closed my eyes. The tiredness weighed me down. It even weighed my eyelids down.

"Are you still here?" I asked Merlin.

"Yes, Alec, I'm here."

"Go away."

"You need my help, dear boy. You wait right there while I get the cure for what ails you."

"Wait," I said.

"Yes?"

"How are the police officers? The ones in the hospital."

"They're fine. I had to sneak past the nurses to apply my poultice but you'll be pleased to know that the two officers are on the mend."

"Good. Now go. I want to sleep."

I heard him go down to the basement. My mind drifted into a black void.

I felt a jolt of energy spark through me like lightning bolt. My eyes snapped open and all thoughts of sleep were gone. I felt as if I'd never need to sleep ever again.

Merlin had placed Excalibur in my hands.

I tried to push the sword away but he put his hand over mine, pinning my hands to the sword's handle. "Don't fight it, Alec. Let the sword feed you. Doesn't it feel good?"

I couldn't deny that it felt good but it didn't feel right. Because I was sure that no matter how much energy the sword gave me, it was also taking something from me. Something intangible maybe but still something of mine that the sword was leeching away.

If the sword made me feel this good, did I care? If not for Excalibur, I'd be out cold right now and in a couple of hours, I'd be waking up with a splitting headache.

This was much better. I settled into the sofa and gratefully received the energy the sword was giving me.

"That's it," Merlin said. "Just accept it."

23

Felicity drove home after visiting the cemetery. When she got inside, she put the kettle on and sat at the kitchen table while she waited for it to boil. Even though her life had fallen apart, she felt happy. She'd helped Jessica Baker and her mother and also any would-be future victims of the man the police had arrested.

Also, after the terrible treatment she'd received at the hands of Nigel Lomas and whoever else he was working with, meeting Charlie Sutherland's ghost had affirmed her faith in human nature. There were good people in the world. Well, not exactly in the world in Charlie's case.

She made the tea and took it into the living room, where she stood at the window and looked out at the street. This wouldn't be her home for much longer. Once she told Nigel Lomas to shove his fake job, she could be sure of that. What was she going to do next? She supposed she could visit her parents in Sussex, stay with them for a while, but that felt like taking a step backwards.

She sipped the hot tea and let her mind wander over the possibilities. She could get a research job, particularly in the field of Egyptology if there were any going. That would make her parents proud as she'd be following in their footsteps.

She could teach Ancient History at a university or college. That sounded okay but she was afraid she might find it boring.

In fact, after everything she'd done while working for the Society, she probably find everything boring.

That didn't leave her many options. It was the Society of Shadows or nothing. Not much of a choice.

She noticed a black van parked up the road. She was sure it was the same one that had been sitting outside the office. Why the hell were they watching her? She went to the kitchen and took a pair of compact binoculars from her handbag. Returning to the window, she unfolded them and trained them on the van.

It was the same van. Her Clairaudience symbol was still there on its side panel.

That gave her an idea. She got the scrap of paper that had the spell on it from her handbag and went out to the Focus. The symbol was still on the radio. The spell had faded away last time but she might be able to reactivate it.

She chanted the words and the same two voices came out of the radio. This time, though, instead of sounding bored, they sounded excited.

"I'm telling you," the woman said. "I saw him. The target. So call it in. Let's get everyone out here and nab him."

"Should we though? What if we take him ourselves? We'll be heroes."

"He's supposed to be dangerous. I'm not sure we can take him."

"What? The two of us? Of course we can!"

"I don't know," she said, obviously considering it judging by her voice. "Maybe we could."

"They'd never put us on shitty stakeout duty again," he said.

"Wait a minute. Maybe they would. If we show them that we're really good at it, then they'd put us on it again. And again."

"Bloody hell," he said. "Maybe we should call the cavalry then."

"Yeah, maybe we should," she agreed.

"Right, I'm calling it in," he said. There was a pause, presumably while he dialed his superiors, and then he said, "This is Oscar Lima Two Zero.

We have seen the target." A further pause, then, "Near her home. He was in a car. A black Land Rover Defender."

Felicity frowned. Hadn't she just seen a black Land Rover drive past? She looked up and down the street. Yes, there it was. Behind her. She couldn't see the driver clearly because he was too far away.

"There he is!" the man in the van said. "The target. He's on this street right now."

The Land Rover accelerated past the van and skidded to a stop next to the Focus. Felicity was out of the car and pulling on the Land Rover's passenger door. She had to know who was inside.

She got the door open and her eyes widened when she saw who was behind the wheel. Thomas Harbinger. Alec's dad.

"Mr Harbinger!"

"Jump in, Felicity. These bastards have made it hard for me to make contact with you so it's now or never."

She got into the Land Rover and closed the door. From her own car radio, she heard the van man shouting, "In pursuit! We are in pursuit!"

Thomas pressed the accelerator and the Land Rover sped away. Felicity checked the road behind them in the passenger side mirror. The van was pulling away from the curb.

"We'll get away as long as they haven't got any friends on the roads up ahead," Thomas said.

"I don't understand what's happening," she said. "Why is the Society hunting you?"

"Because they think I stole something from them."

"Why do they think that?"

"Because I stole something from them. Well, that's not exactly true. It was many years ago and I was acting under the authority of a higher power than any of those idiots."

"A higher power? Do you mean God?" She'd never known him to be a religious man but maybe he had been years ago when he'd stolen whatever it was he'd stolen.

"No, witches."

"Witches? Now I really don't understand."

"All will be revealed shortly."

He took a left and increased his speed. "We just need to lose these bastards first."

Thomas got to the bottom of the road and then turned the wrong way along a one-way street.

"What are you doing?" Felicity asked.

"Losing them."

"Don't get us killed in the process."

"That's the trouble with the Society," he said. "Everyone has had the same training so they think they know what I'm going to do to evade them. That's why I have to do the unexpected."

He checked the rearview. "There, I think we lost them."

"Are you going to tell me what's going on now?"

"Of course. Ask me anything."

"Why did you disappear? We heard you went walking in Hyde Park and just vanished."

He grinned. "Ah, yes, my little ruse. Quite clever. That left them all scratching their heads, I can tell you."

"And us," she told him. "Alec was worried about you?"

A touch of tenderness flickered in his eyes. "Was he?"

"Yes, of course."

"Well, I didn't realize he would be. I'll apologize to him when there's a good time."

"As soon as we stop this car would be a good time," she said.

"No, that's not possible. I can't make contact with him yet."

"Well can I tell him I saw you?"

"No, that's absolutely out of the question."

She shook her head in frustration. She could hardly speak to Alec and not tell him that his father was all right.

"Listen to me closely, Felicity. Not a word of

what we're about to discuss must get back to Alec. Do you understand?"

"No, actually, I don't understand."

"No, of course you don't understand but do you agree? If you don't, I'll drop you off here. After calling a taxi for you, of course."

She wasn't exactly sure what she was agreeing to. And she wasn't very good at lying. The only reason she'd gone to work at Harbinger P.I. at all was because Thomas had hired her to spy on Alec. Her cover had been blown within five minutes.

But if she didn't agree with Thomas, she'd never know what this was all about. Her curiosity won out. "All right, I agree."

"Excellent. I know you're a woman of your word so now we can speak freely."

"Why were the people in that van talking about a prophecy."

"A prophecy?" He seemed to think about that and then grinned. "The clever bastards. They wanted to track me down so they looked up any prophecies about me that might give them a clue as to me whereabouts. This meeting we're having right now is very important so there are bound to be prophecies foretelling its occurrence."

"Really? This meeting?"

"You don't understand what's at stake yet."

"So tell me."

They'd left the city and were driving by the moors. Thomas pulled over and killed the engine. He turned in his seat to face her. "Forget about the Society. It's fallen into chaos and soon it will be nothing more than rubble. A relic of a bygone age. Forget about being a P.I. Soon, there won't be any P.I.s."

"What do you mean there won't be any P.I.s? Of course there will."

He smiled but there was a sadness in his eyes. "The world is about to change, Felicity. This is why I sought you out. I know that you wanted to be a P.I. because you have a desire to help people."

She nodded. "That's right."

"If you join me, you won't only be helping people, you'll be helping to save the world."

She sighed. "I don't know what you're talking about."

"But you're willing to listen to what I have to say?"

She thought about it and nodded. "Yes, I'll listen."

He grinned. "Excellent. Wait here." He opened the glove compartment and took out an item that looked like a Fabergé egg. He got out of the Land Rover and placed the egg on the road. Then climbed in behind the wheel again.

"It'll happen in just a moment," he said.

Felicity had no idea what was supposed to happen.

The egg exploded in shower of blue and gold sparks, creating a portal in the middle of the road. Through the portal, Felicity could see another road, this one cutting through a forest to a large building with many windows.

"Right," Thomas said. "Let's begin." He drove the Land Rover into the portal and it closed behind them.

THE END

For the latest Harbinger P.I. news, check out the Facebook page: https://www.facebook.com/HarbingerPI/

Did you enjoy this book? Please leave a review!
Twilight Heart Amazon Page

44627163R00127

Printed in Poland
by Amazon Fulfillment
Poland Sp. z o.o., Wrocław